W9-ABH-343

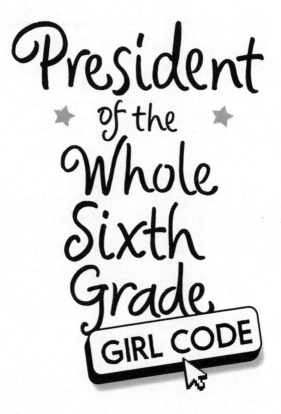

President of the Whole Sixth Grade

GIRL CODE

SHERRI WINSTON

LITTLE, BROWN AND COMPANY
New York   Boston

This book is a work of fiction. Names, characters, places, and incidents are the product of the author's imagination or are used fictitiously. Any resemblance to actual events, locales, or persons, living or dead, is coincidental.

Copyright © 2018 by Sherri Winston

Cover art copyright © 2018 by Erwin Madrid. Cover design by Marcie Lawrence. Cover copyright © 2018 by Hachette Book Group, Inc.

Hachette Book Group supports the right to free expression and the value of copyright. The purpose of copyright is to encourage writers and artists to produce the creative works that enrich our culture.

The scanning, uploading, and distribution of this book without permission is a theft of the author's intellectual property. If you would like permission to use material from the book (other than for review purposes), please contact permissions@hbgusa.com. Thank you for your support of the author's rights.

Little, Brown and Company

Hachette Book Group
1290 Avenue of the Americas, New York, NY 10104
Visit us at LBYR.com

First Edition: March 2018

Little, Brown and Company is a division of Hachette Book Group, Inc. The Little, Brown name and logo are trademarks of Hachette Book Group, Inc.

The publisher is not responsible for websites (or their content) that are not owned by the publisher.

Library of Congress Cataloging-in-Publication Data
Names: Winston, Sherri, author.
Title: President of the whole sixth grade: girl code / Sherri Winston.
Other titles: Girl code
Description: First edition. | New York; Boston: Little, Brown and Company, 2018. | Series: [President series; 3] | Summary: "Working on an assignment for her journalism class, Brianna Justice learns about coding, and the difference between herself and a group of inner city girls"—Provided by publisher.
Identifiers: LCCN 2017037191| ISBN 9780316505284 (hardback) | ISBN 9780316505307 (open ebook) | ISBN 9780316505314 (library ebook)
Subjects: | CYAC: Journalism—Fiction. | Computer programming—Fiction. | Social classes—Fiction. | Stereotypes (Social psychology)—Fiction. | Cheerleading—Fiction. | Middle schools—Fiction. | Schools—Fiction. | African Americans—Fiction. | BISAC: JUVENILE FICTION / Social Issues / Friendship. | JUVENILE FICTION / Social Issues / Prejudice & Racism.
Classification: LCC PZ7.W7536 Pv 2018 | DDC [Fic]—dc23
LC record available at https://lccn.loc.gov/2017037191

ISBNs: 978-0-316-50528-4 (hardcover), 978-0-316-50530-7 (ebook)

Printed in the United States of America

LSC-C

10 9 8 7 6 5 4 3 2 1

R0452157302

To all the teachers at Muskegon Heights Middle
School who always told me, "Yes, you can!"

Reporter's Notebook

January 1. Happy New Year!

Show I'm ready to be the best young
reporter EVER!

1

My name is Brianna Justice and I am president of the whole sixth grade. I am also a businesswoman and cupcake baker. And if I've learned one thing so far, it's that life has to have purpose.

Which is why, when my friends and I had a sleepover to celebrate New Year's Eve, we all made resolutions. And mine was to pursue my new purpose: becoming a butt-kicking TV journalist.

I used to think being a cupcake-making millionaire like my girl Miss Delicious from the Food Show Network was my purpose. I've been baking since I was little. Still love it. Only, now I'm in middle school and I've got so much more on my mind.

A few marking periods of journalism introduced me to a whole new world. Now I have a new hero—Yavonka Steele, *Action News 9*. Her investigative reporting has sent crooks to the slammer and scammers running out of town.

I thought she was The Business. (That means awesome, the best, amazing.)

So, naturally, when I found out that my beloved journalism teacher at Blueberry Hills Middle was assembling a group of professional journalist mentors and that Miss Yavonka was one of them, well...I had to make sure she picked me. TV news is where I want to be!

I even have a plan to start an online bakery so I can save money for journalism school. Now how's that for purpose? My life has purpose all up in it!

At least, that's how I see it.

Soon, Mrs. Galafinkis, my journalism teacher, is going to pair us with our mentors. After she sees my investigative story on the lack of nutritional choices in the cafeteria—I am going to blow the lid right off the mystery meat controversy that has been sending kids to the nurse's office since the first week of school—I know I'll be the number one draft choice. The MVP. The lucky student who gets paired with Miss Yavonka Steele!

You'll see.

It's all going down this week!

Reporter's Notebook

Tuesday, January 2

Notes for Mrs. G.'s class

The basics of being a good reporter!

WHO—Make sure your reader knows who the story is about.

WHY—Readers must know why we are writing about a particular person, but they must also understand "why now?"

WHAT—What has happened?

WHEN—At what time did the event occur?

WHERE—In what location did the event take place?

Brianna's To-Do List:

Must make sure investigative story on cafeteria food is best EVER!

So much to do, so little time!

2

"White girls can't dance!"

That's what my friend Lauren wanted us to believe, anyway. Lauren was killing us with her.... um... "dance moves." We practically fell out of the school bus laughing.

The Michigan air was icy and cold. The ground beneath our feet was a crunchy crust of snow packed over days and days of ice. Foggy clouds puffed all around us, creating frosty breath halos. (Breath halos—that's a metaphor. My language arts teacher would be pleased.) Anyway, we were breath-halo-ing up the place as we tried to recover from all the silliness. We didn't care about our runny noses or freezing toes. Too busy laughing at that fool friend of ours.

Lauren was doing what she called her "white girl

dance," a shady version of an already shady dance move. I was like, "Do your thing, ma." Besides, anybody with eyes could see *this* white girl definitely couldn't dance!

Lauren had her narrow butt tooted in the air, one leg stuck out, bouncing herself up and down. The look on her face was hee-hee-larious—one eye squinted shut like a pirate, tongue stuck out the corner of her mouth, elbows flapping around like she was about to go airborne.

I was laughing so hard I was scared I would mess up my top-bun. You know, a future star reporter and businesswoman needs to look tight and right—always!

Ebony shook her head, tossing her long, thin braids. "Seriously, girl," she said to Lauren, "why so many white girls don't have no rhythm?" Between you and me, I'd seen Ebony dance, and let me tell you, being African American did not help her rhythm at all. Just saying.

Lauren, her blond topknot bobbing with her uncoordinated movements, grinned, pumping her palms heavenward in a played-out raise-the-roof sort of way.

I noticed that our laughter and general rowdiness was drawing unwanted attention from the under-caffeinated, always-bitter Assistant Principal Snidely, who was standing in the doorway to the front hall. Arms crossed. Glowering at us. Throwing major shade, if you ask me.

Red ignored old Snidely. Red, a nickname for fiery-haired Scarlett Chastain, had pulled her petite frame onto the toes of her black leather boots. Chin up and back straight. "I'm a white girl and I have rhythm," she said, twirling down the sloping walkway. A perilous feat, considering the slant of the ground and the ice. But she made it look easy.

"Girl, that is not rhythm. That's ballet," snorted Ebony. "And stop that twirling before the assistant principal comes over here. You know he'll send people to IS in a heartbeat!"

"Then how about this?" Red asked, and before Ebony could even open her mouth, Red did a perfect walkover, delicately placing first her front foot, then the back, on the slick ice.

Ebony hissed, "Cut it out! If Snidely sees you, we'll be in IS for a month!"

In-school suspension. I may have only been a sixth grader, but I already knew too much about it, so I had to bite my lip and make a silly face at Red. Then Ebony tried to quiet her own laughter behind her gloved hands, but plumes of frost hung around her face. Did I mention it was cold? Really, really cold.

Lauren did a shimmy inside her jacket, attempting another ungraceful dance move. She stuck her butt out, then her leg, and—*whoosh!*

She was going...going...gone!

See, our school got its name partly because Blueberry Hills Middle was actually on a series of hills. The back of the property sloped downward. Way downward.

"Omigod!" someone yelled.

"Girl down!" Ebony yelled as we raced to Lauren's rescue. Before we could reach her, Lauren was flat on her back, looking like she was going to make a snow angel.

Then Ebony fell belly-first on the ice, skidding across the ground, barreling right into me. Normally I was very sure-footed, but the weight of my book bag pulled me to the ground.

And who was the only one still standing? Red, our little ballerina!

Now we were laughing so hard, I swear to goodness, I was scared Lauren was about to wet herself. That girl's face was redder than Rudolf's nose.

Ebony pushed up to her knees, pulled out a hairbrush from her book bag, and made this goofy expression.

"Hey, it's ya girl Ebony, coming to you live from the GNN—Ghetto News Network!" I slapped my hand over my mouth, but I couldn't hold back the laughter. I knew it might not be right saying junk like that, you know, making fun of ghetto news or whatever, but she was truly cracking me up.

"Brianna, can you tell me what happened here today?" Ebony's imitation of her favorite ghetto-acting YouTuber, "Go Ask Darnell," was on point.

I played along, giving my answers with a hand on my hip. (Shhh! If my mom saw me acting like one of Darnell's cast members she'd knock me over with her shoe. Okay, maybe not. But, as FBI, she might try to have me arrested!)

With all the clowning around, none of us paid any attention to the large truck lumbering down the hill beside us. Or to the smaller truck at the bottom of the hill.

Until...

A sharp *hiss*!

Air brakes screamed for traction on the slick ground. The sickening sound of large rubber tires whump-whump-whumped, trying to grab hold of some unfrozen earth and finding nothing but ice. The metallic shriek of brakes pierced the air as the long truck body spun sideways and began to skid.

Staring down the hill, watching helplessly as the big truck started its slow-motion pinwheel routine, I realized with horror this was going to get a lot worse. At the bottom of the hill, puttering along, was the other truck.

I looked at Ebony, who looked at me. But it was Red who spoke first. Pointing at the much smaller truck, she said, "Is that what I think it is?"

"Um, yeah! Most definitely," I concurred. *Concur* had been a vocabulary word last week in language arts. So had *calamity*. Which was just a new way of saying d-i-s-a-s-t-e-r!

The smaller truck was one of those clunkers you see a lot out in more rural areas. Junky old trucks with wooden pens for animals.

One minute the large truck was grinding its brakes against the skid; next thing, it had sideswiped the smaller truck with a solid THUNK!

The noise crackled in the cold air. Kids stood frozen like shadowy snowmen.

The smaller truck thudded into the nearest snow-bank, tilting to one side.

Cows made multiple moos.

Only then did I read the big, bold sign emblazoned along the side of the larger truck:

OREOS.

The big cookie truck had just wiped out a tiny truck full of cows!

Reporter's Notebook

Tuesday, January 2

BREAKING NEWS
BREAKING NEWS
BREAKING NEWS

Why is the news "breaking"? When news breaks, does that mean it's broken?

Breaking news is simply an alert to let you know that something new is happening and you need to be aware. Sometimes news can break where you least expect it—even sneaking up on you at your own middle school.

If news breaks and Yavonka Steele isn't there to report on it, is it news at all?

3

For a second, nobody moved. To the east, the sky remained dark, with only a suggestion of the rising sun, a thin pink trail peeking between multiple layers of black and gray.

Seconds passed, and then it was as if we all came back to life at once. Red and I and a seventh-grade boy from my journalism class raced to the smaller truck that had been carrying the cows.

"Mister, uh, sir, are you all right?" I panted against the glass of his rickety old truck as the three of us yanked at his door handle.

"Stop banging on the dad-blasted door!" cried the old man. He unlocked the door and pushed it open. The scent of old tobacco spilled out, along with the bouncy tune of Katy Perry's "California Gurls."

He didn't look like the kind of guy who'd be driving around singing KP. He looked like what Grandpa referred to as an "old codger." Grandpa often lumped himself into that category: grumpy old men who move when they want to and do as they please.

We stepped back and he moved out of the cab, as creaky as his truck. When he stepped onto the slick ground, for a second or two I thought he might spill over like his cows. He did not.

"You like Katy Perry?" asked Lauren. The man's blue eyes flashed like he was thinking, *Don't badger your elders!*

He moved around for a few seconds, making sure everything still worked. Then he looked at Lauren and said in a softer voice, "Me and the girls like all kinds of music." He nodded toward the cows, which had spilled onto a snowbank and were now wandering, slipping over the icy ground. "Miss Katy is one of our favorites, but we like that gal who sings 'bout all the single ladies, too."

The scent of damp hay and cow droppings wafted off the man. A few of us took a step back, except for that one kid. Normally quiet and almost invisible in class, he seemed absorbed by the old man's every syllable.

The guy who had been driving the semi rushed over, his face a crisscross network of worry lines. He was quite a bit taller than the older man, lean-faced, and wearing a black cowboy hat like a bad dude from the Old West.

Both men started going on about how they hadn't seen each other and how the ground was so slick.

The tall man from the Oreo truck had a mustache that bounced around when he talked. His name was Larry, I think.

"Now I got cookies all over the ground," sighed the Oreo cowboy, removing his hat. "What a mess!" The farmer had introduced himself as Cletus. Larry asked if he was sure he was okay and Cletus grumbled about his arthritis acting up and how his wife had been nagging him about getting "the HBO on that danged idiot box," and he said he had a tooth that had been hurting since he saw Frank Sinatra in Vegas for his honeymoon.

Larry appeared to listen to all of this before asking if

any of that was because of the accident. Cletus scratched at his patchy white hair and shook his head.

"Naw, I reckon whatever's wrong with me this morning started going bad long before I laid eyes on you!"

So Larry turned his attention to his Oreo truck. The back doors hung open. The ground behind the truck was littered with dozens of bright blue packages of cookies. Larry put his hands on his hips. Cletus put his hands on *his* hips. I put my hands on my hips. We all stared at the cookies.

"Hey, man, want some help picking up them cookies?" asked a kid who did not have his hands on his hips.

Cookie cowboy Larry put his hat back on, shrugging. "I for sure can't put 'em back on the truck."

"If we pick them up, can we have some?" asked the kid.

"Help yourself," the truck driver said, blowing into his fists for warmth.

In the frozen stillness of the early morning, a voice shouted a phrase guaranteed to reach the ears of even the groggiest kid:

"FREE COOKIES!"

All of a sudden, an avalanche of kids raced from all different directions. Feet stomped, hands grabbed, bodies dove. Shrieks of delight and groans of defeat filled the air as kids fought to nab the cookie packages.

Red edged alongside me and said, "Maybe if we get somebody to go over and milk one of the cows, we could have some milk, too."

"Cow milking is beyond my skill set," I said.

"Brianna! Catch!" called a voice. Just as I looked up, a package of Oreos came sailing at my head. I snatched it out of the air just before it could smack me in the face. Lauren had turned into a cookie quarterback.

We started laughing—first a little, then more, until soon the truck drivers were laughing, too.

Then came the big *MOO*!

I guess it's all fun and games until someone spooks a herd of cows and they start stampeding behind your middle school. Can six cows be a herd?

We learned too late that having a bunch of middle school kids rushing around grabbing up packs of cookies is apparently quite startling to a cow.

That wasn't even the craziest part. A couple of cows wound up in the drop-off line in front of the school. An angry mom in an SUV honked at one of the cows—a big one, with patches of white on her chocolate-brown sides.

It seemed the cow did not like being honked at. So she kindly head-butted the woman's ride.

AP Snidely practically had a heart attack on the spot.

By the first bell, every kid in school had their own version of what had happened, even kids who were nowhere near the accident. Mrs. G. listened intently as several of us crowded around her desk to tell her about the morning excitement.

"It certainly sounds like you kids came face-to-face with breaking news this morning," she said. I thought she was joking, so I laughed. Mrs. G. was only a teeny bit taller than me, with curly brown hair so thick it could terrify even the toughest brush. She wore round glasses over warm brown eyes and thick cardigans with patterns of tiny roses or plaid.

She asked us to take our places. The journalism room was the most unique space in the whole school, and the best, as far as I was concerned. We didn't have desks. Instead, fat colorful beanbag chairs were sprinkled around the area like giant gumdrops. Circular rugs in primary colors made it feel futuristic.

"Reporters, I have a different kind of assignment for you today," Mrs. G. said. We each lowered onto our beanbags—mine was cinnamon red. She sank into one that was bright yellow and smiled at us.

"So much about journalism has been changed because of technology. Technology has changed many career fields like journalism, and created many, many others. So today we're looking at one of the careers that didn't exist when I was your age," she said.

"Did they have dinosaurs back then?" asked one boy. My head snapped up, ready to tear into him for being dumb, but then I caught the smile on Mrs. G.'s face and realized she thought it was funny.

Maybe it was, a little.

She shook her head. "Nope, no dinosaurs. Maybe a DeLorean or two." She laughed. We just looked at her. What was a DeLorean, anyway?

For the next thirty minutes or so, we listened as Mrs. G. talked about new career fields opening up. Since we often talked about how technology was changing journalism, she wanted us to see how tech affected other fields, too.

She asked, "Who here knows what a wind turbine technician is?"

We all looked around at one another because what in the world was a wind turbine? Let alone a wind turbine technician?

A few of us made the mistake of being curious about it and Mrs. G. went on for almost the rest of the class period: telling us how energy generated from wind power, or wind-powered machinery called turbines, was the future, and with the need for wind turbines rising, there was also a growing need for people who could take care of them.

She compared it to air conditioners, saying that after World War II, more than a million American homes got new A/C units. "And somebody had to take care of those things when they broke down," she said with a grin. "It was a new frontier. Today it's wind turbines!"

Her smile was wide and her eyes sparkled like she had just dropped some serious knowledge on us. We love Mrs. G.

But much as I hated to admit it, for the rest of the day, I couldn't help thinking about how the people back then probably thought air conditioners sounded as weird and funny as wind turbines.

That made me wonder. What was next?

I☆I☆I☆I

On Wednesday, Red and I were in our usual seats on the school bus. She nudged me and said thanks. I nudged her back. We'd been working out together, running and stretching and stuff like that.

"I'm gonna get you to change your mind," she whispered.

I giggled. "I don't think so, but I like hanging out at the gym and working out with you. That's as far as I go, okay?"

She shook her head like a little kid. "Nope. Not okay. I'm-gonna-change-your-mi-ind," she sang in a whisper. Oh, brother!

Red was on this kick lately to join a competitive cheer team at her ballet studio. She'd been born with a heart defect and struggled with its effects for years. Now she wanted to prove to herself that she could be as normal as anybody. To her, being a cheerleader meant being normal. We'd gotten to know each other over the past several months and I really admired her. She'd overcome a lot with her heart condition. So I was cool with helping her reach her rah-rah goal.

But she wanted me to join the team with her. Um, Brianna Justice is nobody's cheerleader, okay?

We were still nudging each other and acting silly when a few other kids from our J-class started talking about Mrs. G. and the whole "new technology" thing. This girl from class whose name I didn't know was asking, "Did you guys see the *Blueberry* this morning? Did you see that kid from class on the news last night?"

Ebony leaned across the aisle to share a "Go Ask Darnell" video with me. "What kid?" she asked.

I was trying not to laugh at Darnell. Usually I tried to convince kids I was too mature for such foolishness— and I was. Mostly.

Then the girl whose name I couldn't remember said, "That Julian kid. The quiet one. Did you see him on the news?"

Apparently, while we were all laughing and yukking it up yesterday after the milk-and-cookies collision, one of my journalism classmates was taking names and keeping notes.

I went to the *Blueberry* page, and there it was:

COOKIES, COWS, AND A SWEET MORNING SURPRISE

By JULIAN BERGER

Students won't soon forget the frosty January morning when an eighteen-wheeler filled with Oreos began to skid down the hill behind Blueberry Hills Middle School, slamming into a 25-year-old Chevy pickup full of cows.

"I was just listening to my Katy Perry," said the farmer, Mr. Hamm. "I never even saw that truck coming. Too darned cold to be up. Too early!"

The driver of the eighteen-wheeler filled with Oreos says he noticed the smaller truck too late. "At least the kids helped pick up all the cookies that wound up in the snow from the accident," he said with a laugh.

23

The story continued with quotes from different kids; even Snidely said, "Students at Blueberry Hills Middle should never accept free cookies, especially ones that have fallen in the snow!" That's Snidely for you. He knows how to take lemonade and turn it into lemons.

"It's good, huh?" asked Red.

I nodded, getting a weird feeling in the pit of my stomach. It had never, not once, occurred to me to run, grab my notepad, and report on the incident. I figured between the rumor mill and actual eyewitnesses, the whole story would get told to death.

"Did you ever think about reporting on it? For the paper, I mean," I asked Red. She shook her head, soles of her boots pressed together while she did a familiar stretch.

I went on, "Do you think we should have?"

Red gave me a palms-up shrug. "Lord, I hope not. Because it never crossed my mind."

"Mine either."

I chewed on my lip. Red's biggest wish was to be normal—just like everybody else. But I wanted to be better than that. Reading Julian's story again, I couldn't help thinking about him reporting on a story when no one asked him to. While my friends and I were rolling around in the snow laughing, homeboy was out doing his thing.

Was that what you were supposed to do? Did good reporters just know when to jump in and write a story?

And if so, what did that make me?

Reporter's Notebook

Mrs. G.'s walls are covered with quotes and inspiration about writing, about news, about life. Even though I don't fully understand it, this one feels important:

> "Journalism can never be silent: that is its greatest virtue and its greatest fault. It must speak, and speak immediately, while the echoes of wonder, the claims of triumph and the signs of horror are still in the air."
> —Henry Anatole Grunwald

4

When we walked into class, my friend Click was standing near the whiteboard beside Mrs. G, whose face had that happy-teacher glow. I knew right away something was up.

Click waved me over. He asked, "Did you hear about Julian?" Sigh.

Next thing you know, Mrs. G. is in the middle of a Big-Time Journalism Nerd Fest. Going on and on about what a wonderful thing Julian did and how he was *sooooo* perceptive.

Then she asked us all to join her in giving Julian a round of applause. I glanced over at Red, who gave me a little shrug. My stomach felt bubbly, and not in a good way. See, I didn't mind giving anybody props for doing something good. And I had nothing against Julian. I barely knew him.

But what had me spooked was the fact that he was getting all this praise for writing a story when I had never even thought about it.

All of that was bad enough, but after hearing Mrs. G. explain why Julian deserved all that praise, I didn't know whether to turn in my reporter's notebook for good or just plain run and hide.

"Out of all my students in this class, he was the only one yesterday who thought to grab his notebook, ask questions, and write a story," she said. "Julian, I am so proud of you!"

I had to ask: "So you mean it's all right to interview people and write stories even when they haven't been assigned?"

She clapped her hands together and let out a bark of laughter.

"Absolutely!" she said. "That's the thing about breaking news. No one assigns it. It's all about journalistic instincts, Brianna. Who could have known in advance that a little old man's cow truck would wander into the path of a gigantic Oreo truck?"

I felt my cheeks burn with the hot, hot shame of poor journalistic instincts. Could I get into a most excellent wind turbine technician school? I'd probably have about as good a chance of that as getting into a number one journalism school. I had such big plans for my future. Now, all I can think is...

What if I don't have what it takes?

I ☆ I ☆ I ☆ I

Later that night I couldn't wait until seven thirty, my favorite time every Wednesday. It was when Neptune and I made time to talk.

Frederick Douglass London, aka Neptune, was the lap-swimming tween heartthrob nephew of POTUS— that's president of the (whole) United States! He was also a good friend I'd met several weeks earlier when our class visited the nation's capital.

We didn't have any kind of love connection or what-ever. But I liked him. Really liked him. And I looked forward to our weekly FaceTime chats.

A lot of girls in my position might want to get all goofy in the head about knowing a guy like him. To me, though, he was just a real chill person I could talk about stuff with. Even though we hadn't been friends all that long, I found it easy to ask his opinion and discuss important matters. And I was totally better at *Mario Kart* than he was when we played online together.

I pushed the FaceTime icon on the screen and heard the familiar *bloop, bloop*. The call connected and a face filled the screen. Lean face, close-cropped sandy brown hair, and gold-flecked hazel eyes. Cheekbones that rose when he smiled.

"Hey, Wook! Why'd you change your hair again?" he said.

I said, "Maybe I changed it because I didn't want you calling me a Wookiee!"

"All right then." He laughed. "Well, with it up on top of your head, you look so, I don't know, official."

Ha! I am official.

I did an eye roll and he slouched down. He was on the floor in his room. I was laughing when I reached up, took the bobby pins out of my bun, and shook my hair out until it covered my face.

"WOOKIEE!" he yelled. "You're back!"

"Shut up or I'll pull out that photo of you in your Speedo that went viral!"

30

"Okay, okay. Low blow, Wook!"

So I said:

"Just call me Boss Lady. And that's MISS Boss Lady to you!"

"More like Miss Bossy."

We laughed a little, then I felt my heart begin to thump faster. I couldn't explain why. I'd been waiting all day to tell him about what happened in J-class. Instead, we both let the silence linger, this thing passing between us. This *something* that we didn't understand. Not really an awkward silence, but . . . something.

He looked at me and knit his bushy brows together. When his voice came out, it was softer but also curious. "What's wrong?" he asked.

"Why do you ask that?" Even though something *was* bothering me.

"I can tell when you've got something churning underneath all that hair," he said. "What's going on?"

For a moment, that weird feeling in my chest swelled into something uncomfortable.

Beside me on a large floor cushion was my tiny cat, Angel. She'd butted my face with her nose. I scooped Angel cat into my arms, sighed, and settled in. "Uh-oh,"

Neptune said with a laugh. "Looks like somebody doesn't want to share your attention."

Neptune pulled his long legs into a crisscross position and asked, "Are you gonna tell me what's wrong?"

So we spent the next hour talking about journalism and writing and being the best. I told him about Julian Berger and how he had been able to recognize breaking news while I, Brianna Justice, president of the whole sixth grade, apparently wouldn't know a breaking news story if it bit me on the butt!

"I'm disgusted with myself!" I blurted. Until that moment, I hadn't thought about it, but it was true. I was beyond angry with *me*.

"But why?" he asked.

"Why? WHY?" I was sputtering. I mean, what did he mean, why?

WHY? Well...

Pinpricks of doubt danced along my cheeks, my arms, and my lips.

Yes, *why*? Why had this whole journalism thing freaked me out so much?

"Well, I...I just feel like if there was a news story

around, I should have known it! Instead, I didn't even think about it. I just want to be the best, you know?"

"But why?" he repeated more softly. His tone caught me off guard. The hairs along my arms tickled a little. I chewed my lip and felt the beating of my heart. Was this what doubt felt like?

That sent me sputtering again. "Why? What do you mean, why . . ."

His laugh brought a merciful end to my chicken squawk.

"Cut yourself some slack, Miz Boss Lady. When you were here in December, you did your thing. When my aunt was on the Hill fighting for attention for education funding, you recognized that story potential. What you accomplished was crazy. You helped a United States senator achieve history! How many sixth-grade presidents or journalists can say that?"

Okay, so he had a point. When Mrs. G. explained what it meant and how the senator was trying to do something called a filibuster, I got as many of our classmates as I could to help spread the word. One minute we were passing out cupcakes we'd baked in my uncle's restaurant, next thing we were on TV and the senator had achieved an historic filibuster. The power of that event led me to want a more public platform. As much as I loved cupcakes, I realized that journalism could change lives.

"Look," I began, then laid out my whole plan. How I was less interested in baking for a living and more interested in becoming someone who could change the world, like a journalist.

"You don't have to be a journalist to change the world. Look at what happened a while back with that one girl in New Jersey," he said.

"What girl?"

"She was just a regular kid, you know. I think her name was Mya, Mary...no! It was Marley. Marley Dias. She said she was tired of reading books about white boys and dogs or something like that."

"True, true." I laughed in response.

"Right. So anyway, Miss Marley Dias was a little boss. She started a campaign to collect books about black girls and she donated them to different schools and libraries," he said.

"I heard about her," I admitted. "And what she did

was great. Still, I thought getting into one of the best journalism schools in the country was, you know, my destiny. Did you know that Northwestern University in Chicago, one of the top journalism programs, costs seventy thousand dollars a year?!"

Neptune whistled. "Dude," he said, "that's a lot of cupcakes."

"Dude," I said, repeating his tone, "that *is* a lot of cupcakes!"

We laughed. Then I told him my plans of starting an online bakery to earn and save more money.

"Your mom works for the FBI, right? And your dad is a nurse? Aunt Kaye says there are special kinds of scholarships based on your parents' employer. Just wait, you'll see," Neptune said.

"Easy for you to say. You're the nephew of the president. POTUS is gonna make sure you'll be all right. Meanwhile, I don't want to be an FBI agent or a nurse, so special scholarships based on my folks won't help me!"

"Dang!" He sat back. I hadn't meant to get so worked up. Now looking at him, I couldn't tell if the hurt look on his face was real or if he was playing around. "You sure get vicious when your future feels threatened."

That made me laugh again.

"All I'm saying, Swimmer Boy, is your aunt Kaye is right about the scholarships, it's just getting the right kind. If I want journalism scholarships someday it means getting ready now. Getting Yavonka Steele to mentor me would be a great step in that direction!"

We were both quiet for a few moments. Then he brightened and said, "Well, you've got a little time left, don't you? Before you guys get paired up."

I blew out a long sigh. "No, not really."

"Well, even if all you have is a day, make the most of it. If finding a better story will give you an edge, find a better story."

He ran a hand across his close-shaved head. Then I stared closer.

"Now what?" he said.

"Are you getting... Is that fuzz on your chin?" I drew back sharply and blinked hard. I didn't know why, but thinking about him having man-hair on his face felt weird.

Not to him, apparently. 'Cause that boy's face split into a grin wider than the Detroit River.

"You see it?" he asked eagerly. "Yeah, I have to shave

now. Uncle showed me a few tricks. You know, so I don't get razor burn."

I burst out laughing and shaking my head, but soon realized my mistake. All it took was seeing the totally humiliated look on his face. When I tried to make it better, my words tangled up. (And to tell the truth, I may have laughed some more.)

Finally, I cleared my throat and asked if we could get back to the journalism thing.

Neptune held himself very still for a few moments. I recognized how he managed his stress by managing his breathing. A swimmer thing, I guessed. He said, "How do you know you'll even want to be a journalist when you go to college? Aunt Kaye says people go to college to figure themselves out. You don't have to figure all this stuff out now. You've got time, Brianna."

Out of the corner of the frame, someone entered Neptune's room and spoke to him.

"I have to go," he said. "I know how you are, Brianna. If you want something bad enough, you'll find a way. But for someone with your vision and outlook, have you considered that investigative journalism might not be the end of the road for you?"

Whoa!

"Um, uh, huh? End of the what now?" I said. "Boy, I'm just trying to get on the road, period."

"Sorry. Don't tell anybody, but Uncle likes to listen to old-school R and B when we hang. 'End of the Road' was a song by Boyz II Men. Guess it stuck in my head."

"So you and POTUS just hanging, listening to old soul?" I asked.

"Pretty much, but be quiet. I was making a point. All I'm saying is maybe it's too soon to settle for any one thing. I mean, you're only eleven. Who knows? Maybe what you really want to be is the president. As in, of the whole United States."

We both thought about that for a second. "You mean, maybe one day I'll be in the West Wing, eating chips and listening to slow jams from back in the day?"

"Just keep an open mind about the investigative journalism thing, that's all. Who knows? You might find something else you like even better. In the meantime, why not find another story to investigate. Something that ol' LaTonka Steele can't ignore."

"Um, that's Yavonka Steele."

"That's what I said," he replied with a wicked grin.

He was about to push his END button, when he said, "Oh, I wanted to tell you, Aunt Kaye and I are coming to Michigan in February."

"Why?" I asked.

He shrugged and said, "Not sure. Some kind of First Lady stuff for President's Day. A meeting with some politicians. I'm hoping we can hang out. I'll be in touch. Later, Bossy."

"Later."

Reporter's Notebook

Thursday, January 4

Mrs. G. says a reporter is only as good as her questions. Tips for good interview skills:

1. Be prepared. Know something about your subject before your interview, if possible. Do your research.
2. Always ask the basics—what is happening, when will/did it happen, who caused it to happen, how did it happen, and why?
3. Never end an interview without asking the subject if they can think of anything important that you should know but didn't ask.

5

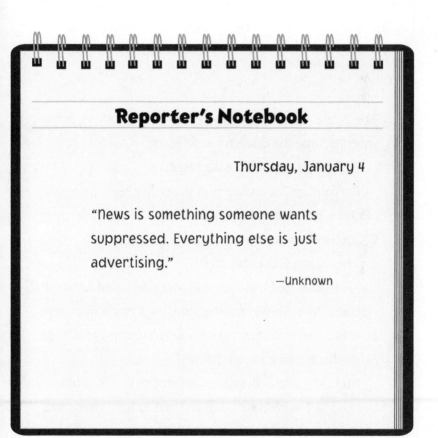

Reporter's Notebook

Thursday, January 4

"News is something someone wants
suppressed. Everything else is just
advertising."

—Unknown

6

The entire school-paper staff, plus several others, were crammed into the *Blueberry* newsroom.

"What's going on?" I asked Red.

Even before she answered, I knew. My heart dropped. No time for a new story now. It was "The Mystery of Cafeteria Food" or nothing.

The mentors had arrived.

"Now that we have distinguished guests and honored visitors," Mrs. G. was saying, nodding toward our principal and mentors, "join us once again in congratulating Julian Berger for a job well done!"

Mrs. G. stood beside our principal. Mr. Striker, big and tall with hands larger than lunch boxes, was grinning from ear to ear. Alongside him stood several grown-ups I didn't recognize.

Except for one.

A tall, cinnamon-brown woman with high cheekbones and intense brown eyes. A short haircut that looked sleek and sophisticated and a navy pantsuit with pale stripes. It was my all-time favorite investigative reporter, Yavonka Steele, *Action News 9*.

I felt a lump in my throat. I wasn't ready. I. Was. Not. Ready!

My gaze raked over the other mentors. I swallowed hard. My in-depth nutritious lunch story definitely didn't seem strong enough anymore.

I felt desperate. Yavonka Steele had to pick me. She just had to, right? Right?

Wrong!

Yavonka Steele stepped forward and said, "We all discussed it and agreed, Julian, little man, you are the best choice for me. Julian Berger, would you be my partner?"

I was so numb. I barely even heard when my name was finally called.

Not by Yavonka Steele, either. It was a youngish-looking man. At least, I thought he was behind that thick brown mustache and trendy hipster beard. *Groan!* And he was wearing a sweater-vest and a bow tie. A bow tie, y'all.

"...Matthew McShea, but you can call me Matt," he said. His hand was extended, I realized, waiting for me to shake it.

The greatest, crime-busting-*est* reporter in all of Detroit was over there huddled up with her "little man," and here I was, at the mercy of Hipster McSweater Vest.

"Um, I mean, hi," I said, shaking his hand. "Nice to meet you."

Lie! Lie! Lie. You know what would be nice? Getting paired with Yavonka Steele, that's what would be nice!

McSweater Vest grinned wider. He also wore large, black glasses with plastic frames. Hmm...I wondered if his nose and mustache were attached to the glasses.

My brain couldn't process everything that was happening. Mrs. G. was still going on about Julian's greatness. Then she told us we'd need our parents to sign permission slips to allow us to ride in the car with our mentors.

"They'll pick you up tomorrow after school," she said. "Instead of working in the newspaper room here, you'll work with the professionals in their newsrooms or studios. Isn't that great?"

Yeah, greaaaaaaat.

Could I stand his chipper hipness long enough to learn anything? He wasn't even an investigative journalist, like Yavonka Steele.

Part of me wanted to quit.

❘☆❘☆❘☆❘

When I walked into the journalism room the next day, I spotted McSweater Vest, wearing tan cords and a tan, cream, and brown rust-striped vest over a cream-colored shirt. The sleeves were pushed above his elbows. He didn't spot me right away because he was playing with his phone.

I moved quickly out of his line of sight and spotted who I was looking for.

Yavonka Steele.

She was sitting with Mrs. G. to the far side of the room, and they were both holding cups of coffee. Last night, I decided I needed to find out exactly why she picked Julian and not someone else. Like yours truly, for example.

"Um, hi, excuse me," I said, clearing my throat.

"Oh, hello, Brianna. Yavonka, this is one of my brightest young students, and president of the whole sixth grade, Brianna Justice."

"Oh, a politician, eh?" said Yavonka.

I felt myself stand taller. Okay, so Mrs. G. does think I'm one of her brighter students. I reached out my hand and Yavonka Steele took it in hers. She had a firm grip and cool fingers despite holding the coffee cup.

She said, "Look at her with that hair bun high and tight, and that crisp white shirt. She looks like an executive. Well, it's very nice to meet you, Miss President!" I liked the way she looked right at me, giving me her full attention.

I wanted to play it cool; instead, enter the crickets sound effects. 'Cause ya girl was scared silent.

I just stood there. Mouth open. Eyes rolling back and forth.

"Madam President," said Yavonka Steele with a sly grin, "may I have my hand back, please?"

Did I mention it was getting awkward? I dropped her hand.

"Brianna," began Mrs. G., "did you need something, dear?"

I closed my eyes for a second. Took a deep breath. Glancing from one to the other, I blurted:

"Miss Steele, I am a huge fan of your segment on the news and hope one day to follow in your footsteps, which is why I did an investigation into the mysterious ingredients in some of our lunch items. I mean, if a girl can't trust her school lunch, how can she be expected to learn and eventually become a productive member of society!" *What?* I was babbling. Miss Steele's eyes got bigger and she wore what could have been an amused look.

Or a cry for help!

"Sure, honey, I remember your story," she said. My heart leaped in surprise.

"Did you think it was good? I mean, no offense to anyone, but I really wanted to work with you. I feel like our styles and personalities would, you know, mesh well together."

Mrs. G. let out a hoot of laughter.

"Ha! She's got a point there, YaYa!" Mrs. G. said.

YaYa?

She must have caught the questioning look in my eyes, because she said, "Yavonka and I were college roommates at Michigan State. And you do remind me of her." This brought a fresh round of laughter between the two of them.

"Are you saying she's driven like I used to be?" Miss Steele said.

Mrs. G. pulled a face. "Used to be? Girl, please!" she said.

Now they were laughing full out. It was weird watching Mrs. G. act like a, well, you know. A regular person wearing a Spartan hoodie and going to college football games. It was blowing my mind.

I was so busy yukking it up with Mrs. G. and my news idol that I didn't see McSweater Vest until he was right up on me.

"What's so funny?" he said. When he smiled, the ends of his mustache quivered.

What Yavonka said next stopped my heart cold. I was dead. Worse than dead. I was the living dead.

President Zombie.

"I think your mentee is trying to ditch you," she said between laughing fits. I felt all the blood drain from my face. I didn't want to hurt McSweater Vest's feelings. At that moment, I just wanted to disappear!

Please, somebody, run down to the science room and build me a time machine. I need to go back ten minutes and start this over.

My eyes were shut tight and I wanted to back away. But I felt a hand on my shoulder holding me in place. When I finally opened my eyes, I saw it was McSweater Vest. He was smiling.

"By the time we're finished working together, she won't even remember your name, Steele," he said.

"Uh, no, um...it's not like that. No offense, Mr. Sweater, I mean, McShea, sir. I mean, well, I just really wanted to know how the mentors picked their student partners. I really want to be a TV reporter. Why did Miss Steele pick Julian and not, um, someone else?"

"You mean, why didn't she pick you?" Mrs. G. said, wiping laugh tears from the corners of her eyes with her fingertips. She said to Yavonka, "See, YaYa. Told you she is a lot like you. A real go-getter."

Yavonka Steele stood straighter and tried pulling together a more serious face. She nodded at Mrs. G., then turned to me and said, "That is an excellent question. I read your cafeteria story. And the story you wrote a while back about the little girl with cancer. I've read all your stories, I believe."

Yavonka took both my hands in hers. Looking right at me, she said, "I deal in two kinds of news—breaking and stories that allow me to investigate and dig deep. My favorite is a story that offers both.

"The ability to recognize when news is going on around you is critical for a journalist. Out of all the kids who submitted stories, Julian was the only one with the instincts to react to what was going on around him and recognize its news value," she said.

Seeing the look of total hopelessness on my face, Yavonka said, "Honey, don't worry. Whether you start out in print or not, the rules for getting good news are the same. But especially in TV you have to work fast and think on your feet. You'll get there."

And that was that. I felt woozy and sick. If she didn't think I had what it takes now, how could she be sure I'd "get there"? Was she trying to give me hope? Or did this mean I didn't have what it takes to be a real investigative journalist?

Reporter's Notebook

Friday, January 5

Notes from Mrs. G.'s board

Do

1. Keep an open mind.
2. Be respectful.
3. Ask follow-up questions.
4. Finish all interviews with, "Is there anything else you'd like to add?"

Don't

1. Make promises you can't keep. (e.g., "This story will run on the front page...bring you more business...save your job.")
2. Assume anything. Take nothing for granted.
3. Belittle your subject.
4. Give up!

If I don't get my act together, I'm not going to need the online business to pay for J-school. I'll need it to support me!!! Wonder if I can create a website for a business I haven't even started yet.

7

Icy pellets of snow ticked against the windows of McSweater Vest's car.

The entire world was pale white and pearl gray as traffic moved along the M-10. We were almost downtown, approaching the tunnel at Cobo Center and Joe Louis Arena. Whenever I saw Joe Louis or Cobo, I knew I was downtown.

My gaze shifted over to McSweater Vest. He had been talking to me about the story he wanted me to work on. Something about inner-city girls and computers. If I did a good job, he said, the story would get published in the newspaper.

I didn't have the heart to tell him that getting into the

paper or the online edition was fine, but I still wanted to be on TV!

McSweater Vest parked and the two of us rushed inside a huge gray cement building. He was chattering about how it used to be the Federal Reserve Building. He said the famous Free Press Building on Lafayette had been sold to some big investor.

Inside the blocky building was like something in a magazine. You couldn't help feeling a little important in a place like that. Stone and glass shimmered beneath overhead lights throughout the lobby area. Huge windows revealed fat flakes of snow falling noiselessly from a colorless sky.

A big dude whose name tag read J. sat on a stool. He wore a green blazer that bunched up around his massive arms.

My trusty mentor flashed his ID badge and J. smiled. He looked at McSweater Vest and said, "McShea, didn't know you had kids." J. looked at me and grinned.

Hmph! So J. works the comedy circuit on the weekend, right? He's got jokes.

McSweater Vest released a short laugh, his cheeks, already cherry red from the cold, turning even redder.

"J., my man, this is Brianna Justice. She goes to school out in Orchard Park and I'm her mentor."

J. cocked a brow. "Orchard Park, eh? Fancy!"

I didn't know if he was trying to be funny or not. I had never thought of Orchard Park as fancy.

Not wanting to get off on the wrong foot, I smiled. "Nice to meet you," I said.

J. nodded and said, "McShea is one of the good ones. Be nice to him. Y'all take care." He stepped aside and we moved past him toward a group of elevators.

"This is the newsroom," said my mentor when the doors finally opened. We walked into a wide-open space. The windows overlooked Fort Street. Pearly gray daylight blended with the glare of overhead lights.

I looked around the space and felt a ripple of excitement.

"We're back here," McSweater Vest said, leading me deeper into the space. People glanced up, gave me a look, then went back to doing whatever.

"This area is called the city desk," he said. "Not an actual desk, per se, just a way of characterizing what we do. All of us report on various aspects of the city—crime, courts, education, government, categories like that. You can drop your stuff right here. No one's using this desk right now."

I dropped my bag on the floor and removed my heavy coat.

"Sooooo, if it isn't the Bearded Boy Wonder and his new protégée. We could use some new blood around here," said a voice. I turned and found myself looking at a big, round dude who was using his swivel chair to move across the room.

If I were giving out nicknames, which I was in my mind, his would be Ginger Bear. He was pale and freck-led, with curly reddish brown hair, and hands like bear paws. He had happy blue twinkly eyes.

He held out one hand for me to shake. "I'm Buffalo Bob, nice to meet you. Ol' Matthew told us he was bring-ing a student in today. What's your name?"

"Brianna Justice," I said. A black T-shirt stretched tight around his belly. I squinted at the light brown outline of a woman's features superimposed against the darker back-ground. Beside the woman's silhouette, the shirt read:

"THE MOST COMMON WAY PEOPLE GIVE UP THEIR POWER IS BY THINKING THEY DON'T HAVE ANY."

—ALICE WALKER

"Do you know who Alice Walker is?" He peered over the top of his wire-framed glasses, challenge in his pale blue eyes.

"Yes, I know who she is," I said, proud of remembering how Alice Walker was one of my late grandma Diane's favorite authors. "She wrote *The Color Purple*." I couldn't help wondering why this big white dude was wearing a shirt with an African American author's face on it.

"Do you know what the quote means?" he asked, crossing thick arms over an ample belly. I glanced over at McSweater Vest, who looked like he was about to jump in. Maybe he thought I needed help. I didn't.

"Um, I think so, but I don't understand why anyone would just give away their power," I said. "That's stupid!"

"That's the point," said Buffalo Bob, leaning forward in the chair. "They don't think they have any power. It's about people who feel powerless."

I shrugged. "Well, that sounds like giving up to me. If you go around acting like you don't have power, don't have control, then I guess you don't."

He grinned, then said, "Well, all right, little mama." Then he drummed on his legs, ready with another question:

"Do you believe people who have power are more important?"

A woman, tall, thin, and wearing no makeup, with hair the color of blue cotton candy, came around the corner.

"Buffalo, don't get started on the kid. Sweater Vest is trying to be a mentor. Don't go scaring her."

Well, I guess I wasn't the only one who couldn't stop looking at his goofy vests.

"Nice, Liz. Way to teach our young charge to respect my authority," McSweater Vest said.

She rolled her eyes. "When you talk like that, Sweater Vest, you make me hate you and your funny wardrobe."

I stifled a laugh.

Then Buffalo Bob practically barked, "Hey! Knock it off. I was in the middle of a very important interrogation of this budding journalist."

He swiveled back to me. "If she wants to be in this business she oughta be able to voice her opinions. Am I right?"

I drew a deep breath, blew it out. "I'm not afraid to give my opinion or whatever. Answering your question, I think powerful people are not more important than anybody else. It's just that being powerful means they've got more people to listen to them and say they're right."

It's weird. There's something about talking to grown-ups treating you like a person—and not just some dumb kid—and challenging you to think, like they are really listening to you. It's exciting. Talking to Buffalo Bob made my heart thump faster, almost like being on a game show. Like *The Life Show*, where the questions are based on important stuff and not something lame. I liked the feeling, even if it was a little scary.

The springs in the big man's chair squeaked as he leaped from the seat. "Somebody give that girl a gold star. Matt, I think this one'll give you a run for your money."

I found myself grinning.

McSweater Vest pointed at him and said, "Bob, get back to your side of the room and leave me to mentor this bright young mind."

Buffalo Bob saluted, dropped into his chair, then put it in reverse and rolled away. Liz tugged a loose strand of powder-blue hair away from her face and gave me another look up and down.

She looked at my mentor and said, "Are you sure the two of you didn't go to school together? She almost looks like she could have been in J-school with you, Matt!"

I☆I☆I☆I

Over the next hour, I actually found myself interested in McSweater Vest's career.

He'd graduated from Northwestern's School of Journalism six years ago. That made me sit up a little. They were the number one top journalism school in the country. I was dying to ask how he'd paid for such an expensive school, but thought maybe that would be rude.

Instead, I listened.

He told me why he enjoyed writing features. How a lot of breaking news or even investigative journalism pieces moved so quickly that they ignored what was most important—the people who were affected.

"Your first assignment is all about impact," he said.

He pulled up a flyer, all jazzy and colorful, onto his screen:

Come to the computer coding and design event of the year geared toward girls of color.

SHECODES!

January 27, 9:00 a.m.
at the Lakeside Sports Complex.
Computer literacy is important to your future.
Why not start now?

Participate in one of two tracks:
1 Basics and coding in app creation
2 Webpage design

Join us for an exciting day of technology and fun with local industry leaders and educators!

Special Guest Appearance by
Sen. Madeline Wilson-Hayes

Girls can do
ANYTHING!

The conference was coming up in about three weeks.

I frowned at the flyer, recognition dawning. "It's the conference the senator told me about when I met her in D.C.," I said.

"Exactly! That's why I knew you'd be perfect for this story!"

I felt my entire body groan.

Okay, so back in D.C. I did help the senator draw attention to her cause. It wasn't hard. I believed in her passion, fighting for more funding so schools could up their technology game.

What she was doing seemed cool and all, believe me. But I'm not a big technology kind of person. If it weren't for Neptune giving me one of his extras, I wouldn't even have an iPad. My old clipboard was just fine. (Okay, don't tell anyone, but my iPad is slightly more fun than my old clipboard.)

Still, the idea of talking technology with a bunch of girls I don't know from a shady neighborhood does not sound like great journalism. It sounds like a big yawn to me. Just the idea of computer science or coding or whatever was making me want to nap. For sure I'd never get Yavonka Steele's attention with tech news!

"Programs like SheCodes expose girls to science in a way their schools cannot. It's also about more than just teaching them the basics of computer coding or website building," he said. "It's about introducing them to the knowledge that there is a bigger world full of opportunity beyond the poverty and hardship of their neighborhoods."

"But I don't know anything about computer coding or disadvantaged girls," I said, speaking slowly.

He grinned and said, "Aha!"

If he pulls a rabbit out of his drawer, ya girl is out!

Thankfully, he was rabbit free.

I wasn't trying to be snippy. What kind of disadvantage was he talking about? Instead of asking that, I asked why black girls need special programs more than others.

His answer: "Indeed!"

Huh? I didn't want to be rude, but y'all, I couldn't help rolling my eyes. Still, he just laughed.

"Trust me," he said. "That is an excellent question. Do African American girls *need* access to computer science more than anybody else? Or, is it that without some intervention, African American girls living in low-income areas might never *have* access?"

I just looked at him. He said the girls were from low-income families. So when he's talking about these girls being disadvantaged, he's talking about being poor or living in poor neighborhoods.

He smiled like he understood what I was thinking even though I was sure he didn't. He said, "That's where research comes in. And not just online research or from books at the library, either." Uh-oh. The way he looked all excited, I was scared of what was coming next.

He continued, "I've arranged to take you to Price Academy, a charter school on the east side, where several girls signed up for the SheCodes program. I want you to interview them."

Whoa!

I felt a little *thump-thump-thump* pulse in my neck. Was I excited? Or terrified?

He slid in front of his computer and pulled up a file. It was a list of names. Then he produced a permission slip and told me to have it signed before he picked me up at school the next day.

"If your parents sign the approval slip, I'll have permission to pick you up at lunchtime next Tuesday. That way we can spend the whole afternoon at Price Academy."

He also said that since many other mentors and mentees were partnering up, I could pick a partner, too, if I wanted.

"Can I think about it tonight?" I asked.

"Absolutely!" he replied with too much enthusiasm.

Hmm...

I wasn't totally sold, but I wasn't ready to give up, either. Maybe a partner was just what I needed.

Reporter's Notebook

Friday, January 5

*McSweater Vest told me to start researching STEM careers as well as careers in computer science.

A woman named Katherine Johnson, born in 1918, worked as a human computer for NASA. Her contributions, as well as those of other African American women scientists and mathematicians, were featured in a movie, *Hidden Figures*.

never heard of black women working for NASA or being part of the country's first spacewalk. Why is that?

Potential online bakery names:

- Planet Cupcake
- Amazing Cupcakes
- Star Cupcakes
- Out of This World Cakes and Goodies

8

"McSweater Vest wasn't my first choice."

I was talking to Red, Lauren, and Ebony the next day as we headed to our science class. "However, that doesn't mean I want to do less than my best. Besides, a story on disadvantaged kids could make Yavonka Steele take notice!"

"Girl, be warned. You know when they say 'disadvantaged,' they're talking about those bad kids in the ghetto. I'd take a bulletproof vest if I were you!" Ebony said.

"I don't think that's true!" I said defensively. But I had begun to worry that was exactly what *disadvantaged* meant.

Ebony clicked around on her phone until she found a meme. It showed a picture from an episode of *SpongeBob*

SquarePants where he'd done something dumb to everybody in Bikini Bottom. The whole town was chasing him with torches and pitchforks, looking like zombies. So SpongeBob was running like his life depended on it.

The text under the photo read:

When you take the wrong exit and wind up in the ghetto, you be like…

GET ME OUTTA HERE!

I laughed, then instantly felt guilty. It wasn't like ghetto was a curse word. So why all of a sudden did I feel funny laughing at it?

Red, ignoring the running SpongeBob, said, "Well, I think working with him will be good for you."

"Why? You think—" I began.

She cut in: "I think the kind of story he has picked for you sounds awesome. I'm so glad you invited me to be your partner. My mentor is a dancer. He's a great dancer writing for a dance magazine, but he doesn't care at all for actual journalism. Other than getting tips on my grand jeté, I don't think he'd be much help. What you need to do, Miss Brianna, is relax and be open-minded."

"Uh, hello? I'm open-minded!"

"Justice, you know, you can be sort of…um, rigid!

Like a grown-up. You know how you want things and you just expect them that way."

Well!

"Rigid? What does that mean?"

Ebony giggled. "No offense, but you're just, you know, really, really mature-acting. Sometimes I feel like I'm your student and you're our sub or something. And since Christmas break you've started dressing like a young professional. You know? Prepped out."

I gave her such a side eye. *Hmph!* Rigid! *Me?*

Lauren gave a bark of laughter and high-fived Ebony. "Nice save, Eb," Lauren said. Then, to me, she said, "I love your new young executive look. It's so you. But c'mon, Bree, I've known you since forever. You've always been a little more serious and dedicated than the rest of us. Now, with your striped cardigans and crisp white shirts, you look the part. Luckily for you, preppy chic is in."

"Preppy what—"

I didn't get to finish that thought. Instead, as I rounded the corner I crashed right into Jorge Milian.

"Dang, girl!" he said. Jorge was a trip. Long body, skin like caramel. Even though he was fussing because I truly did bump into him, he was also grinning.

"Come on, Cupcake Girl, you know what time it is!"

A chorus of voices, including Red's, piped up:

"It's Ugly Cake Friday!"

Okay, so Friday mornings I start my day at Wetzel's Bakery. My friend Raymond's mom owns the bakery. She found out I liked to bake and she offered me a place to sell my cupcakes.

It's been great, but I want to also sell my cupcakes online. Mom says I am stretched too thin already. *Hmph! We'll see about that.*

On Fridays I bring the bashed-up, smooshed-up cupcakes and experimental baking treats that didn't make the cut for the display case. Between you and me, sometimes I make a few batches and just smoosh 'em and ugly 'em up to bring in anyway.

Thank goodness I didn't forget to bring the box this time. As we entered the classroom, everybody hovered around me like I was carrying gold. The bell rang, but our teacher was still a no-show. All you could hear was "mmm-mmm-mmm" and "num-num-smack-smack-smack."

Jorge held up a golden cake with what looked like spikes sticking out. "What was this one supposed to be?" he asked.

"I was trying to mix praline into my batter, but I couldn't get it to act right."

He laughed, held his head back, dropped the baked confection down his gullet, and said, "It's acting right now!"

Everybody was still eating and munching when Ebony shouted out:

"Hey, y'all, Brianna Justice is going to interview some East Detroit kids. Not downtown east, but eastside east, as in, sho' 'nuff ghetto."

Jorge grabbed another chunk and grinned. He said, "Brianna Justice goin' to the hood!"

Everybody burst out laughing. I laughed, too, but I didn't feel like laughing. They were starting to make me nervous—scared, even. I didn't like not knowing what to expect or how to act.

We were eating and laughing so much that we didn't even notice that our teacher was so late. Finally, thirty-five minutes into the class period, the sixth-grade dean came into the classroom and announced that our science teacher was not coming to class—EVER!

Dean Carter wouldn't tell us why our teacher left the school. Instead, she passed out some boring assignments. I leaned over to whisper to Red.

"So will you? Partner with me and McSweater Vest for our journalism project?"

She'd been licking a red lollipop. The kind with gum in the middle. She bit into the gumball.

"Well, remember, I'm willing to partner up with you, Justice, as long as you do something for me."

I shot her a look. Not this again. The cheerleading thing. Really?

"You help me, I'll help you?" she said, raising one brow.

I groaned. "Red, you're not seriously going to blackmail me into trying out, are you?"

"Yep!" She grinned.

"But I am not a cheerleader," I argued.

"You will be after the training workshop," she said. "It's gonna be like a cheer boot camp—learning stunts, flips, and routines." Ooo, boot camp. Should I bring combat boots and a Swiss Army knife?

Then Dean Carter said something that sounded a lot like "wonk-wonk, wonkedy-wonk-wonk!"

Since I'd become fluent in school wonk, I knew it meant "no talking, read your assignment, and don't disturb me with your petty requests for hall passes."

"You said you only needed someone to work out with. Now, haven't I done enough?"

"I want you on the team!" Red said, crossing her arms.

"Red," I said, her name coming out like a whine. Dean Carter glanced over her shoulder. I lowered my voice. "C'mon. I'm not the cheerleader type."

"What exactly is 'the cheerleader type'?" Red asked.

"You know. Girls like the ones in those movies who get all worked up about rah-rah-rahing all over the place. Based on what I've seen, they can be very...uh, witchy."

"You watch too many movies. Cheerleaders are athletes!" Red said.

I gave a snort. "No, they aren't."

She matched my snort with an eye roll full of challenge. A look that said *we'll see, girlfriend* all up in it. She followed that up with a long, slow smile.

"I can just see Yavonka Steele begging you to be her co-anchor and BFF after your interview's big splash in the *Free Press*," Red said, in a teasing song. Like a big na-na-nee-na-nah! Her drawly voice made the taunt sound musical.

Dean Carter cleared her throat. No one clears their throat quite like a bored administrator. When Red and

I looked up, Dean Carter pointed her glare at us, so we settled down and read the assignment.

Instead of continuing to fight with Red, I tried reading the worksheet. But my mind kept drifting back to the SheCodes event and the story we were going to write. Since learning of my assignment, I had done a bit of research online. I had no idea that at least fifty percent of all jobs required some kind of computer knowledge and in the next decade that'll increase to more than seventy-five percent.

That got me to thinking about McSweater Vest and our talk about girls in disadvantaged neighborhoods. With so many careers in the future requiring computer training, it makes sense that everybody needs to learn how to use them.

While finishing the worksheet, I realized I had so many questions, but there was one question no one could answer:

Where in the world was our science teacher, Mr. Castle?

I☆I☆I☆I

"Daddy, when's Mom coming back?"

I was pouring Cheerios into a bowl.

"She'll be here next Sunday," he said, eyeing me from behind the morning edition of the *Free Press*. "Why?"

"No reason, just miss her." I put on my best "good daughter" grin. He grunted. I sloshed milk into my Cheerios and scooped a spoonful into my mouth. Operation Get Mom to Say Yes was a go. If I was going to start my own business, I had to convince Mom first.

And that was going to take a secret weapon!

(Evil laugh—wah-ha-ha!)

Even though I might not want to be a baker forever, I still loved it. And earning my own money was *fab-u-lous!* But the last time I talked to Mom and Dad about letting me have an online business, Mom said, "Absolutely not. You're too young and your father and I have too much going on right now to help you make a success of it. Maybe in a year or two when you're a little older!"

"Dad, did I mention, I'm loving your fashion choices this morning?"

He was wearing a Detroit Red Wings T-shirt with red flannel pajama bottoms and a heavy wool coat unbuttoned over his morning ensemble. The mud-brown hat with furry earflaps was a nice touch, too.

He smelled like cold air and wood smoke. He'd been

up since the crack of dawn smoking meat in this big wood smoker. He kept moving back and forth between the rear deck and the kitchen. He looked like a cartoon character.

"Thank you, brat," he said, raising his spatula and waving it around like a king with one of those scepter thingies. "If I were you, I wouldn't get too mouthy. Did you read that permission paper I had to sign for your cheer boot camp whatchamacallit? My first car didn't cost that much!"

I tried to hide a giggle. In order to go to the boot camp, parents had to submit signed permission and a check to cover the cost of competing should their child make the team. Was it wrong that I was secretly hoping to give his check back?

"Sorry, Daddy!" I said, batting my eyes and trying to look super innocent. "I could have paid some of it."

He said, "Don't worry, you'll pay some. But Mom and I agreed to do it, so it's done."

One thing I knew for certain: If you wanted to distract parents from money talks, all you had to do was bring up school.

So I told him about Mrs. G.'s quest to teach us about

different careers. Then I surprised us both by asking, "Daddy, did you always want to be a nurse?" My spoon tinged against the side of the bowl.

Daddy gave a little bark of laughter. "Ha! When I was young like you I thought I was going to be a racecar driver. And then retire from racing and open up my own chicken and waffle joint.

"I was gonna call it Dragstrip Diner," he said.

Then he let out one of those laughs old men sometimes do, mouth open, tongue out, all while he chortled, "Hee-hee-hee!" With a very dramatic snap of his fingers, he said, "Girl, I was going to be in business!"

I shook my head. "That sounds so ghetto, Daddy. For real."

He gave me the Dad Squint. His tone was playful, but his eyes were serious. "What've we told you about calling stuff 'ghetto'? Better not let your mother hear it." With a grumble, he added, "I don't want to hear it again, either."

It wasn't a bad word, but I kept my mouth shut. I took another scoop of cereal. Milk sloshed. The spoon tinged the side of the bowl. Wood smoke swirled on the outside deck.

He shook his head, his face taking a thoughtful

expression. "You know, to answer your question, when I got to high school I wanted to be a doctor," he said.

"For real?"

My dad was the kind of guy who liked cooking, grilling, hanging out with his old-dude friends, and sometimes taking car engines apart and putting them back together again. I'd never pictured him as someone with dreams of being anything other than who he was.

He nodded. "I joined the navy when me and your mother married. The plan was to apply to medical school when I finished my service while your mother went on to join the FBI."

"What happened?" I scooped the last bits of cereal out of the bowl and into my mouth.

He smiled. "Your sister happened. We wound up starting our family a little ahead of schedule." He looked sheepish.

Katy! Wouldn't you know it. She was causing trouble before she was even born!

He said instead of medical school, he finished with the Navy so Mom could go to FBI training.

"Dad, do you sometimes wish you could still be a doctor?"

He did a little shrug. "Sometimes, baby. But, well, it'd take at least a few more years to pull that off. And it's not cheap. So, well. . . ."

He let his voice drift off, then stood and started toward the door. He stopped, palm on the handle, and turned:

"You know what, brat," he said. "It's nice having breakfast with you like this. I miss you when you are at the bakery."

"Well, Daddy, it's been nice sharing this father-daughter moment, but I've got real life waiting on me this morning." I said.

"Stay outta trouble, brat!" he said, heading for the smoker.

"Sure," I said. "I'm thinking of hot-wiring a car and going drag racing, you know? So I can be like dear old Dad." I snorted out a laugh. It was fun joking around with him.

Without even looking up, he got me back. He said, "Be sure to take the phone book with you. You'll need it to see over the steering wheel."

Short jokes. Really? If I weren't so confident, that would really hurt.

Dad gave me a stiff salute. I saluted him back.

I watched him walk away. As much fun as I have playing around with him, I never thought about him having hopes and dreams. A doctor? You know? I could see it. He would have made a really good doctor.

I stood for a moment, staring at him. What did it feel like to have a lifelong dream and see it disappear? It made me feel bad for Dad. It did something else, too:

Thinking about Dad giving up his dream made me want to stick to my plan and make my dreams come true even more. Which meant getting Mom on board with my online bakery idea.

Operation Get Mom to Say Yes continues!

I☆I☆I☆I

Monday was a teacher in-service day—they had to go to school, but we didn't. With my permission slip and check in hand, there I was at boot camp.

I expected it to be easy because I was used to doing real athlete stuff like basketball in the winter and track, swimming, and tennis in the summer—not jumping around and shaking my booty.

But after two hours of cheer boot camp, my booty

wasn't shaking, it was cramped tight into a little ball. Cheer boot camp was no joke.

Then Coach Tamar decided that because of my size I could be an excellent flyer. That's the girl they throw through the air.

Brianna Justice. President of the whole sixth grade. AND a human cannonball!

When Coach Kristy finally tooted the whistle to say we were done, I felt myself panting with relief. My whole body hurt *sooooo* much.

"Gather round!" she yelled.

Red and I flopped onto the floor beside each other. She laid her head on my shoulder. Her hair smelled like sweet shampoo. I laid my head on hers. We could feel each other's hearts beating. I still wasn't crazy about the idea of being on a cheer team, but seeing that slightly dizzy, happy look on her face made me feel good. I wondered if she'd always feel like she had to prove herself because she'd been born with a bad heart.

She looked up at me and made a face. I stuck out my tongue. We laughed a little. One of those goofy friend moments that happens too fast even to selfie.

The coaches said everyone did an amazing job and

we all made the team. Red squeezed my fingers. I spun toward her, my mouth dropping open. Oh, snap! It had really happened!

"Justice, you should see the look on your face. Girl, you're a cheerleader now!"

"Oh, no!" I wailed. But we were being silly and it felt good, even if it would take some getting used to. I thought about Dad's check. Dang! I might have to wash his car a few times and be extra nice, otherwise he could make me pay him back with my money!

But when the coaches passed out the bags and jackets, I couldn't help feeling a flicker of pride. It would almost be worth paying for myself. Almost.

"We know the fees for participating are expensive, but they include all your gear. Wear them with pride, girls," Coach T. said.

We were all slipping into our jackets and looking inside the bags when Coach Kristy said, "I like to save five or ten minutes at the end of each practice to allow my girls a chance to chat and get to know one another."

She left us and I found myself saying my name and talking about who I am.

"My name is Brianna Justice," I said. "I go to

Blueberry Hills Middle and I'm president of the whole sixth grade. Oh, and our journalism department is doing this mentorship program and Red and I are partners."

Then Red said, "And our mentor is taking us to Price Academy in East Detroit to talk to a group of girls over there and our story is going to appear in the *Free Press*."

Several faces looking from me to Red and back again. A few covered their mouths with their hands.

"NO!" several shouted. One said, "You can't go to Price."

Sandra Poe, destined to be our team's captain, whispered conspiratorially, "Brianna! Red! I thought you guys said you were journalists. Don't you watch the news? The east side is like, well, the gateway to hell!"

Well, that seems harsh!

One girl leaned forward, her voice a foreboding whisper. "I know all about that neighborhood. My dad told me. He's a lawyer!"

Not understanding, I glanced at Red, then pushed on. "Um, no big deal. We're just going to talk them about a really cool program that teaches computer coding and stuff like that," I assured them. Then a different girl grabbed me into a big hug. Soon the others followed and I felt like I was being squeezed to death by sweaty pink anacondas!

"Price has metal detectors and its own SWAT team," said a girl with wide-set blue eyes and shoulder-length blond hair. She made a little shiver. Her name was Lori.

An African American girl named Diandra Mack had her curly hair pulled up on top of her head. She wrapped her arms around herself like the idea of going to the east side of Detroit made her very cold.

She said, "My mom says all the kids over there are just thugs and hoodlums. It's so ghetto. Be careful, you guys, honestly!"

Not once had I given any thought to the girls at Price being different because of where they lived.

Maybe I should think about it. Sure the area is poor, but the kids were just kids, right?

Reporter's Notebook

Tuesday, January 9

"Preconceived notions are the killers of honest observation. Never trade what you think you know for what you can discover."

—Mrs. G.

All right, Mrs. G. I understand what you're saying, but does this really mean I need to be a cheerleader? Hmm...

I HAVE SO MUCH TO DO!

Having a website is expensive!

It can cost anywhere from $600 to thousands!!!

Business Name Ideas—

- Cupcake Diva
- Short Stuff Cupcakes & Treats
- Snack Shack
- Motor Town Munchies

Hmm....I'll keep thinking

9

I tried *not* to think too much about the warnings.

Do you know what happens when you try *NOT* thinking about something? All you do is think about it.

So of course, when I got home, I googled Price Academy. At first, it looked like any other charter school in Detroit. Until stories of fights, arrests, and a whole lot more started popping up.

Omigod!

I said to Grandpa, "My friends say the people on the east side are ghetto. I'm doing this story about a computer coding program for girls from that neighborhood. So is it? You know, poor and kind of dangerous, I mean."

Grandpa was sipping his morning coffee. He used to

be a city cop back in the day. He just shook his head. "The east side? All of downtown Detroit is 'the east side'? Whatchoo talking about, Brianna?"

"You know the part over by Price Academy and that other high school with all the fights? That part. Is it, you know, dangerous?"

"Baby girl, your parents have raised you in a nice, safe bubble. You don't know nothing about 'the ghetto,' as your friends call it," he said, looking up from his church shoes that he was polishing. Black stains smeared on his fingers. He touched his nose and left a smudge mark on one side.

He went on. "What has your mother told you about calling stuff 'ghetto'? Think before you speak, Brianna."

Gawd! Why was everybody so hung up on that word?

"But maybe it's just a word, Grandpa," I said.

He shook his head. "Sometimes a word is so much more than that. Them folks on the east side are no different from you and me except... well, some of 'em have lost their way while others have just simply lost their jobs."

When I looked at Grandpa, though, his expression was sort of sad. Shaking his head like I didn't get it. I hesitated, wanting to say more. But what? I didn't call anybody ghetto, but I knew what it meant when someone said it. And if they were saying it in a funny way, I laughed.

Only now, thinking about the girls at the cheer camp, how they reacted, it didn't feel so funny. It felt bad. But it was like, if I admitted it was wrong, I was saying I'd done something wrong when I really didn't think I had.

"Anything else?" he asked, peering over the top of his glasses. I shook my head.

"Love you, Grandpa," I said, giving him a hug. He hugged me tight.

"Me too, kiddo."

I☆I☆I☆I

On the car ride Tuesday with McSweater Vest, Red sat in back; I rode up front while he went on and on about our upcoming interview, which he now said was more like a "meet."

I couldn't concentrate. I just kept watching the road. Highway 10 was an icy ribbon that looped into downtown Detroit. Glittering high-rises, shimmering beneath softly falling snow like castles of ice, filled the rearview mirror. The tall, shiny buildings gave way to warehouses of red brick, then warehouse buildings with boarded-up windows. We turned onto a street with puddles of melted ice pooling along the curbs. Dirty snow pressed against buildings. Warehouses turned into regular houses. My hands were clenched. I realized I'd been holding my breath.

Then I saw that the houses were...just houses. Some areas had boarded-up windows or abandoned lots, but that kind of thing happened all over Detroit.

Just as I was starting to exhale, to breathe, we rolled up to a stop sign across from a liquor store. I recognized it—this store had been in one of the news videos where a fight had turned deadly. Men stood around, their hard eyes glaring beneath knit caps. It was the SpongeBob meme all over again.

My throat started to go dry.

News images once again popped into mind—cops, crime scenes, and people crying. I told myself, *Brianna, stop trippin'*.

But I must not have been listening. I'd been in all kinds of neighborhoods—good and not so good—and it had never fazed me before. But now, all I could hear in my head were the jokes and the laughter about people who live in places like this.

I shivered.

What was I afraid of? Just because kids lived on the east side didn't mean they were any different from anybody else, right?

A few more turns and we were inside the gated parking lot for Price Academy. Something about hearing the mechanized black iron gate click shut behind us gave me the willies.

Inside, the halls were noisy. The smell of cafeteria food wafted in the air. It felt a lot like our school. Still, a knot was forming in my throat. What if I said the wrong thing? Did the wrong thing? Were the kids here really more dangerous than other kids?

I could hear Ebony's voice in my head:

"You know when they say 'disadvantaged,' they're talking about those bad kids in the ghetto. I'd take a bulletproof vest if I were you!"

McSweater Vest shook hands with an armed guard. The guard seemed to know him. He guided us to the school's front office. I looked at Red to see if she was feeling as unsure as me, but she seemed her usual self. Our mentor stepped inside the office. Red followed. I lingered in the hallway, watching the faces of students.

I caught the eyes of two boys who were staring. They cut their eyes away from me and I heard one ask:

"Who's she supposed to be?"

The other one, making sure he was facing me, so that I heard, growled out, "'Cause she from some school in the burbs she probably think she all that. She just another ghetto girl trying to act like she so different from the rest of us!"

It was like being kicked. He needed to get his facts straight!

The same boy kept glaring in my direction, like he was daring me to say anything, and the knot in my belly tightened. I looked away. So unlike me. Usually, I'd glare right back. But I didn't. I looked away because I felt ashamed. I swallowed hard. I looked at these kids in this busted-up school, kids with skin brown like mine, kids with reputations for being tough or dangerous.

I wasn't ashamed to be black. But I was ashamed of anyone thinking I was like the black kids at this school. Why was that?

Feeling ashamed felt wrong, though. But I wasn't comfortable here. I didn't want anyone to think I... belonged here. In Orchard Park, where I grew up, our grade school was new and updated; Blueberry Hills Middle had its old parts, but basically it was two schools now—the old side with the new. One look told you this building hadn't been updated in decades.

"Brianna!" Red whispered. I snapped out of the dark thoughts invading my head and stepped inside the main office.

A large black woman with coffee-brown skin and a wide smile greeted us. "Well, hello there, Mr. McShea. Glad to see you come visit me today." She gave a playful, almost flirty smile. McSweater Vest grinned. Clearly this flirting was something they did often.

The woman asked, "And who do we have here?"

She looked at Red and me. We both smiled. By now my heart was jackhammering in my chest. I felt nervous and afraid of saying the wrong thing.

McSweater Vest introduced us and we told the woman, Mrs. Gilly, that we were working with him to interview some of their students.

A lady came from down a long hallway and walked up beside us. She smiled, too. Slender with intelligent eyes—eyes like a teacher. She had short natural hair and hazelnut skin with a little pink blush on her cheeks.

"I'm Talia Newsome, co-founder of SheCodes," she said. "I'm so happy you girls could be here. We've decided that rather than sticking you in the conference room all afternoon, it might be good for you to meet in the science lab instead."

Two girls appeared behind her. Miss Newsome introduced them. "Brianna Justice, Scarlett Chastain..."

"Red, please, ma'am. Y'all can call me Red."

Miss Newsome grinned and so did the two girls behind her. "All right then, Red, I'd like you to meet Shania Murphy and Christyanna Webb."

We shook hands with the girls and said hey, and then we were all led through a hallway crowded with students. We got a lot of long stares from people. I tried to make myself relax. Told myself they're just like kids at Blueberry Hills Middle.

Inside me, though, a little whisper asked:

But what if they're not?

I☆I☆I☆I

As Miss Newsome introduced us to the entire class, I felt their stares tickle my skin. With my hair swept up and my clothes tidy and pressed, I wanted to come across like someone who was organized, smart, and ready for action.

Looking around the room, though, I realized that most students wore basic uniforms of navy pants or skirts with light blue or white polo shirts. I touched my hair self-consciously the way I sometimes did when I got nervous. Was I overdressed?

"...so I'd like you to remember what Principal Horton said at the assembly yesterday," Miss Newsome was saying. "When we have guests, we what?"

"Show them our best," came the loud chorus from the twenty or so kids in the room.

Then silence. Everybody was looking at me. And Red. I was pressed so close to the chalkboard, I wanted to melt into it. My throat felt dry. My eyeballs were glued to the floor. Beside me, Christyanna whispered, "Whenever we have important people come to the school, Principal Horton has a short assembly to remind us how to behave. Like he thinks we're gonna embarrass him!" She gave a snort of laughter.

They had a special assembly just to discuss us coming here? Really? For some reason that really scared me big time.

"Hey, y'all. Thanks for having us," said Red. "I'm

just the backup reporter. Uh, Brianna, uh, Justice"—she nudged me, hard—"is the main reporter. We just want to observe the class, I guess, and then talk to y'all later."

"Where're you from?" a kid asked Red. He leaned forward, a suspicious grin on his face.

"Texas," Red said.

"Ha!" he declared. His grin turned into a megawatt smile. He turned to another boy beside him. "See, bro! I knew it! My cousin lives in Texas. He sounds just like her!"

Red laughed. The boy laughed. His "bro" laughed. I tried to laugh, but it felt like my mouth was stuffed with cotton balls.

What is wrong with me?

Then sweet-faced Shania, with her reddish brown curls, turned her pale brown eyes in my direction and totally put me on blast.

"Brianna looks scared," she said. She and Christy-anna were still at the front of the room with us, but she had craned her neck around to see our faces. Now she was staring right at me with a playful smirk on her face. Several kids laughed along with her. Even their teacher, Mr. Hardaway, chuckled.

Then he said, still smiling, "Enough of that, now, let's be kind to our guest."

He told us we could all take seats. Shania moved closer and took my hand, smiling—the kind of smile you give someone when you feel sorry for their stupidity. She said, "Don't worry, girl. It might look rough on the outside, but we watch out for each other in here."

A girl named Shakira said, "Girl, where'd you get that bag? You're a cheerleader?"

I glanced wildly from Red to Shania to Shakira, trying to figure out what was going on, until I realized she was talking about our Detroit Divas backpacks.

Her voice shifted from playful to wishful. Shakira confessed, "I wanted to try out for them, but I was scared that because of where I come from, y'all would be like, 'don't let no east side chick up in here—she might steal our shoes 'n' junk!'" She laughed hard, too hard, and Shania laughed and said, "Girl, you crazy."

Well, that felt awkward. But once again, Red saved us.

"Honey, just because some of those girls have money, don't mean they're not shady. Don't let something like that keep you from joining."

Shakira smiled. She said, "Well, it's not just that.

My mom called for me. Being on that team costs a good chunk of change."

"That's cheddar, y'all," Shania said with a grin. "Cha-ching!"

The three of them laughed, but I couldn't help thinking about how easily my parents had agreed to cover my costs—even though I had my own money.

We settled in and Mr. Hardaway started the class. He stood and asked, "How many of you ladies and gentlemen have ever written computer code?"

Several hands shot up. Even Red's. I was one of the few people who didn't raise a hand. A girl sitting in the back row, a quiet girl with dark eyes, looked at me, glared, then buried her face in her books after lowering her hand. She had light-brown skin and big brown eyes. She was a little chubby and wore a blue winter coat.

Mr. Hardaway went on. "Anybody in here know what computational thinking is?"

Red and I exchanged glances. I sure as heck didn't know. A look around the room revealed that no one else did, either. Then I saw that several students were looking in one direction. Toward the back of the room at the girl who'd given me serious stank face.

"Come on, Alicia," said the dude's bro. "We all know you know the answer."

Shania crossed her arms and smiled at me, saying, "Alicia is like a human computer. She always knows the answer!"

"No, I don't," grumped Alicia. After a second, she sighed and said, "Computational thinking is, like, the way you formulate a problem so that a computer can answer it. It means to come up with a way to tell the computer what to do, you know?"

Soon as she finished talking, her cheeks turned bright pink, then she ducked down her head like she was hiding.

The boy leaned forward and tapped Red's arm. "Hey, Texas, in case y'all didn't pick up on it, Alicia is very shy."

"Shut up, Lamar!" Shakira said with a headshake.

Laughter floated around the room.

Mr. Hardaway continued making his point. The more he spoke, the more I found myself becoming interested in coding. When he paused and asked if there were any questions, I raised my hand.

"Does this school have a STEM program?" I asked.

The science, technology, engineering, and math program called STEM had been in my elementary school. I'd been involved because I liked math. But I had been more interested in money math than computer math.

At Blueberry Middle, I hadn't given STEM a second thought. Now I was wondering if I should.

"No, our school does not have a STEM program at the moment," Mr. Hardaway said. "But we are working on it."

Mr. Hardaway went on with his discussion and I started looking around the room. The bulletin boards were colorful with pictures and charts and diagrams.

Then I realized all the scientists on the walls were people of color, several I'd never heard of. I whispered to Red, "Did you know there were so many black scientists and inventors in history?"

She whispered, "Justice, you're funny." Now, what the heck did that mean?

I asked Mr. Hardaway if I could get up and take a closer look at the faces that lined the walls and bulletin boards. He said sure and I moved to make my way slowly around the room. Each description spoke of the person's background.

Funny. I came here to write a story about science, but I was learning history, too.

Some of the names and faces I recognized from bulletin boards at my own school. It was usually around Black History Month that our school paid extra attention to the accomplishments of people of color. Our boards had all the names and faces everybody knew—from Dr. Martin Luther King Jr. to Malcolm X to Maya Angelou.

Here, however, were some names and faces I didn't recognize:

Dr. Charles Richard Drew, inventor of the blood bank; Garrett Morgan, inventor of the traffic signal and the gas mask; Mae Jemison was the first black woman to travel into space.

And there were still more—Percy Lavon Julian, a chemist and pioneer in drug synthesis and other research that changed medicine. Lonnie George Johnson, an inventor and engineer who invented the Super Soaker and other things. And Marie Maynard Daly was the first black woman in the U.S. to earn a PhD in chemistry.

"She's the one who inspires me," said a girl who'd

come up beside me. I was so lost in reading the boards, I hadn't seen her.

"Hey, I'm Venus," she said before turning back to face the images on the wall. "There are so many black people working in science and technology. It's funny. When the media or those people on YouTube talk about us, they never mention our scientists or our contributions."

I cringed.

She raised an eyebrow, her gaze digging into me. She folded her arms across her body like she was ready to do battle. She said, "I guess jokes about being ghetto are funnier than jokes about being a black chemist or engineer or computer scientist."

Okay, was I wearing a sign that said HEY, I LOVE "GO ASK DARNELL"? It was like she knew I was one of the people who sometimes laughed at those jokes. Venus said she was in eighth grade and that her family was working real hard so that they could afford to move to another part of the city before she started high school.

"Mama says I can't go to school over here if I want to get into college," she said.

"Why?" The question just popped out. She looked

at me hard for a second, narrowed her eyes, and then finally smiled.

"You really don't get it, do you?"

I shook my head. She was silent for a moment, and then she nodded her head toward the bulletin board.

Venus said, "Those fools on YouTube making all their so-called funny videos about black folks in the 'hood.' Just because you don't find a lot of college degrees over here doesn't mean people don't want more. That's why Price Academy tries so hard to push us. 'Cause a lot of people in our neighborhood look at college like you're talking about going to the moon!"

My back stiffened. She sounded like Mom and Dad.

She added, "But I bet somebody like you got us all figured out, huh?"

Instantly, I felt defensive. I got a hot flush on my face, and my jaw clenched. So I stepped to her, said, "First of all, Blueberry Hills Middle is far from fancy. And stop acting like you know me, because you don't."

Her eyes blazed. Our voices were low and hushed, but Mr. Hardaway glanced in our direction and frowned. Body language was telling on us. One look and anyone could see we were in war mode. Still, we both took a step back. I took a deep breath. I wanted to come across as cool. You know? Chill.

I failed so hard.

"Besides," I went on, "so what if a few people think 'Go Ask Darnell' or stuff like that is funny? It's not a big deal, right?"

Oops!

She let out an unfriendly snort. "*Hmph!* Is that so? When you live here and are constantly being called 'ghetto girl' or being made fun of, trust me, it stops being funny real quick. Jokes perpetuate the stereotype. Yeah, per-pet-u-ate. I know my A, B, C's and my 1, 2, 3's. Girl, nobody wants to be made fun of just because of where they live. But with all your money and so-called education, you're too dumb to realize that."

Mr. Hardaway called for us to be seated, breaking the spell between me and Venus. Did she just call me dumb? Really?

I felt like I was breathing fire, but I checked myself. Then Miss Newsome reentered the room and said we were going to a conference room for refreshments and to talk.

Venus, looking satisfied with herself, said sweetly, "I'll see you in there. Maybe I can educate you on what it really means to live in a 'ghetto neighborhood.'"

I☆I☆I☆I

Red and I spent the next hour listening and taking notes.

Daija wanted to attend SheCodes because she loved cartoons and hoped one day to get into animation. Christyanna wanted to create websites. (Hmm...that could be useful!) Venus wanted to create medical apps to help sick people.

Several of the girls said they loved just tinkering around and finding out about stuff. A sixth grader said jobs were hard to come by in their neighborhood and her dad had a hard time finding work after he lost his manufacturing job.

"My mama said if I get an education I won't have to struggle like my family does. She says life will be better for me," another girl said.

Then a girl raised her hand and introduced herself as Tiffani Botti. What she said made me snap my head around and look directly at Venus, who was already staring right at me.

103

Tiffani said, "If I learn computers and get real good at it, maybe when people find out I came from the east side, they won't treat me like I'm nothing. Sometimes it's hard being a black girl in this neighborhood."

I swallowed hard.

Isn't *ghetto* just a word? I always thought of it as more funny than mean, at least the way I used it.

But now—in this school with kids who get called that word all the time because of where they live—I wasn't so sure.

Reporter's Notebook

Computer science is about problem solving. Computer science is everywhere. There is not a profession or an area that is not supported by or touched by computing. And we are natural computer scientists.

In fact, children are some of the most brilliant computer scientists (and scientists more generally) because they are naturally curious and want to understand how things work and the steps needed to make them work in particular ways (e.g., algorithms).

Could someone—even me—design a program to determine why I feel so bad even though I'm not sure what I did wrong?

Feel real icky about even thinking the word *ghetto* now, let alone saying it or watching a video.

Dr. Jakita Thomas is a Philpott-WestPoint Stevens Associate Professor of Computer Science and Software Engineering at Auburn University in Auburn, AL.

Online Biz Names
- Digital Cupcakes
- Cyber Cakes
- Yummy Bytes

10

It took a few seconds for his face to come into view.

"Wook!" cried Neptune from the iPad screen. "I saw this and thought about you!" Then he shook a twelve-inch action figure of a Star Wars Wookiee doll in my face. Well, in the camera lens pointing at my face.

Sigh.

No matter where they live or who they are, some-times a seventh-grade boy is just a seventh-grade boy.

"Real nice," I said, trying to hide my grin. "I hope you didn't buy that with my tax dollars."

He made a horse laugh. Or more like a donkey laugh.

"Nope! Bought this with my allowance. It's been hours since I had Uncle dip into the tax coffers to buy me toys."

Oh, brother!

"Look, are you finished? Because I've got really important business to discuss. I've been waiting all day to tell you about it," I said.

He set aside his toy, crisscrossed his legs and big feet, and said, "Go!"

After our talk the previous week, I'd felt bad about laughing at his boy 'stache. I wanted to make sure that this time I behaved better. After my trip to Price Academy, I felt like I needed to prove I could be a good person.

I drew a deep breath.

"First, tell me about your swim meet. How'd you do?"

And just like that his face got all bright and happy. He told me all about how he'd won the breaststroke and the freestyle, and how this kid from a rival school tried to get in his face afterward.

"I'm picturing some geeky, skinny little prep school white boy trying to act tough over a swim match," I said, laughing.

"Uh, he's black," Neptune said. "And as big as a football player."

Oops!

Was I doomed to be a serial stereotyper?

"Sorry," I said. "Guess that's what happens when you jump to conclusions. I wanted to talk to you about my interviews. I think they went A-MAZ-ING!"

"Cool!" he said.

I paused. "But I met this one girl, Venus. She seemed really smart, but she had attitude to spare. She had the nerve to say I was dumb!"

"You! C'mon, now, Wook. You're a lot of things, but dumb is not one of them."

I felt pleased that he had noticed.

"So what did you say to make her think that?"

"I told her that *ghetto* was just a word and that sometimes the people on the Internet or who make their little jokes or memes are just being funny. I mean . . . I don't do it. But sometimes they can be pretty funny."

He paused a few seconds before speaking. Meanwhile, in my bedroom, Angel cat was rubbing her whiskers against my knee.

"I used to think they were kinda funny, but Aunt Kaye made me take a step back and realize that there's a bigger message," he finally said.

"What bigger message? I mean, I wouldn't take the time to make one myself, but some of those things are funny."

"Funny and making fun of someone are two different things. When you hear the word *ghetto*, who do you see? Like in your mind, who do you visualize?"

Seconds passed, my heart jabbing at me. Why did I feel so defensive? Why did thinking about whether or not to say some word matter? When I used to think of the word, the first thing that came to mind was:

" 'Go Ask Darnell'!" I yelled.

"And in his videos, who is he making fun of?"

My answer came quick. "Those black girls who—"

"So," he cut in, "when you think of *ghetto* you think of black girls in certain neighborhoods."

"Yes, girls or guys who act a certain way. Loud. Aggressive." I could hear my tone. I was practically pleading with him to see where I was coming from. However, the more I listened to myself, the less I liked what I heard.

When I was laughing at those videos with Ebony or my other friends, I was also doing something else— drawing a distinction between how I saw myself and how I saw others, specifically other black kids.

Basing thoughts and feelings on what you've heard

instead of what you know about a person or group is stereotyping. Is that me?

I wasn't like that, was I?

It was just jokes, right?

Still, I didn't like losing at anything—even arguments, so I said, "I'm not wrong. It's not a bad thing if I laugh at something that a bunch of other people are already laughing at anyway!"

"That's lame, Wook." He shook his head. I decided to change the subject. I'd had enough politics for one day.

And with that, I removed the band from my up-bun, took out some bobby pins, then shook my Wookiee-like mane 'til it covered my face.

There was a brief moment's hesitation, then we both burst out laughing.

After a few minutes of that silliness, I told him, "I'm back on track. Now all I have to do is convince Mom to let me start my online bakery before I'm forty and I'll be on fire."

He looked at me for a long moment.

"What?" I demanded.

"You know, your mom could be right. You're into a

lot of stuff right now. It won't be the end of the world if you have to wait a little longer to crush the online business world with your talents." He sounded playful enough, but I could tell there was something serious in his tone.

"So you think I can't handle it?" I snapped.

He held his hands up, palms out, in surrender. "Hey, hey, hey! Don't bite my head off, Wook. I'm just saying, I mean, I haven't known you all that long, so it's not my business, but..."

"But what?"

He cleared his throat. "But you get excited about the idea of stuff sometimes before you really think it through. Your mom has been gone a few weeks. Maybe as soon as she gets back isn't the right time to spring your 'secret weapon' on her, whatever that is."

Boys! They just don't get it.

"Don't worry. I know my mom. I just need to be real smooth with it. I have my talking points all worked out."

"Talking points?" Now he was smiling again. "Sounds like you're going on *Meet the Press* Sunday."

In a way, I was. Only it was Mom who was going

112

to meet the press—me. And like a good reporter, I was going to bring her the facts!

I☆I☆I☆I

Thursday night cheer practice was brutal. Afterward, the coaches gathered us together and told us that a month from the coming weekend, we would have our first exhibition.

The girls cheered and I found myself grinning, too.

Red flopped down beside me, huffing and puffing as hard as me. "Still...(*pant-pant*) think...(*pant-pant*), cheering is too wimpy, Justice?"

All I could manage was an eye roll. When we pulled our sticky selves off the floor and went to get water, a few girls from the team stopped us in the outer hall.

Lori threw her arms around me. "I'm so glad you girls didn't get murdered at Price," she exclaimed.

Then Tracy, who introduced herself to Red and me with a selfie in front of her big house, said, "That place is full of hoodlums and hood rats." Tracy had her arms folded and her meanness on high. Venus's face popped into my head.

"So ghetto," agreed Sandra Poe.

Red looked really ticked off. Before I knew what to say, Red was saying, "Hey, that place isn't that bad. The kids and teachers were great. The students knew their stuff. Have any of you ever been there?"

Tracy took a huge step back.

"Girl, you couldn't pay me to go over there!" she said.

Lori, forever passing out hugs that no one asked for, was quick to throw an arm around Red and me. Then she said, "Don't worry, Brianna. You or Tracy aren't anything like those kind of girls."

"Like what kind of girls?" I asked, my tone low and suspicious. What was she saying? Then I gulped, thinking about how I felt when that boy in the hall at Price said I wasn't any different from them. I knew what Lori meant, and I didn't like it.

So when I felt myself boiling in anger toward Lori and Tracy, I wanted to scream. What right did they have to pass judgment on anybody?

Bright and bubbly as you please, Lori said, "You know. The ghetto kind of girls. The girls who live on the east side. We know you and Tracy and the African American girls here are nothing like, you know, those girls."

She smiled, but reading my *eyes about to pop out of my head* expression, Sandra piped in:

"You know, the kind of, um, girls who live in the grimy part of town."

In her best Texas drawl, Red purred, "Y'all seem to have an awful lot to say about a school and a neighborhood you've never visited. Now, let's get back to practice before Coach T. decides to come and teach us the definition of some other words, like laps, or burpees."

We all groaned, then raced back inside the gym. Running laps was bad enough, but burpees were soul crushing. Still, I'd have rather done a hundred burpees than have to deal with what I was feeling.

Even as I lay awake in my bed that night I stared at the ceiling thinking about the last few days. I was excited about my story, even if I had been afraid to go to Price.

Then I got there and was happy to meet everybody. Yet, I had to admit to myself that I was uncomfortable. But I'd already formed an opinion about the kinds of people who lived in that neighborhood, who went to a school over there.

Only, I hadn't expected to feel so—I don't know—connected and disconnected, at the same time.

When thinking about how bad the neighborhood was, I had sort of had the attitude that if they didn't want to live there, maybe they should just move.

After talking to the girls and interviewing them, however, I found out most came from families that had suffered tough times—job losses, health problems, and a lack of opportunities. Being poor doesn't make them bad people; it just means they have fewer choices.

Angel cat's purring grew almost loud enough to drown out my thoughts. Almost.

The knot of something ugly burned the back of my throat. Remembering how wrong it felt to have the cheer girls going on about how Price was full of hoodlums.

How they were quick to tell me and Tracy we were different because we didn't live over there. They meant because we were black. They meant that because we didn't look like what you expected to see in the "ghetto."

And I thought about Venus. Shania. Shakira. Lamar. Alicia. Just kids. Living their lives like me. People with hopes and dreams for the future. Human beings, not memes.

I fell asleep picturing the strong, beautiful contours of Venus's face. The dark eyes that open with pride when discussing black scientists or become fiery when discussing her neighborhood. And remembered the hard glare from the shy yet assertive Alicia.

Red had been the one to stand up to the little Price poison-party at the gym. I just stood there, mouth open, still trying to defend something I wasn't sure I could defend anymore.

Reporter's Notebook

Sunday, January 14

To-Do List:

- One month to get ready for cheer exhibition
- Two weeks to finish journalism story
- SheCodes Event, 9:00 a.m. Saturday, Jan. 27
- Three shifts at Wetzel's bakery this week!
- OPERATION ONLINE BAKERY starts today!!!

11

Mom was coming home.

I helped Dad, Grandpa, and Katy clean the house and get ready.

For her and my secret weapon!

Around noon, Mom arrived smack in the middle of Dad watching the highlights of Michigan's big win over Michigan State from some bygone era. Dad was so absorbed in the sports rerun, I thought he might not tear himself away from the good ol' days long enough to greet her.

He pulled himself together, though. After a bunch of hugs, we took off for brunch. We went to a popular spot in Orchard Park where they played live jazz music and sometimes gospel, too.

Soon as we got our food and sat down, Katy and I were practically yelling to be heard.

"Girls!" Dad said. "Let your mom breathe. She's barely been home an hour and you two are going at her like hyenas!"

The last part was almost shouted, which was unfortunate since the music had stopped. Several people turned and looked toward us, then returned to their pancakes and sausage.

"That's okay," said Mom with a shine in her eyes I hadn't noticed earlier.

She had news. A little prickly feeling at the back of my neck, with hairs standing on end, told me something was up with her.

Mom was only a little taller than me, which meant that for a grown-up woman, she was short. She exercised a lot—I worked out with her sometimes. She was well toned, like Coach T., and a lighter-skinned version of my caramel-brown self. I knew her face like I knew my own. And right now, my own face was saying, *What's up?*

I had been so focused on my news, it never occurred to me that Mom might have news of her own.

She drew in a long breath and slowly let it out.

Dad, who seemed to be in la-la land somewhere, finally looked at her, too, and saw what I did.

"What?" he said.

Silverware tinkled as she lightly placed both hands down on the table. She stared down at her hands.

We stared down at her hands.

I believe the waiter walking past stopped to stare down at her hands.

She wore a big smile. Her eyes looked watery, like she might burst out crying with all her news.

"I got offered a promotion!" she said in a rush.

"Mom! That's so excellent!" I said. "More money?"

She swatted me with her large linen napkin. Then she winked. "Lots more!"

"Woo-hoo!" I cried.

Katy and I were already calculating the increase in our allowances. Well, I know I was. Then I realized Dad had gone silent. Mom turned to face him slowly. Now her smile was timid, and she was tensed up in that way that people are when they're expecting something.

Dad asked one simple question. Four words that, once out of his mouth, I knew could change my life forever. Four words that Mom, no doubt, was anticipating. He said:

"Is it in Detroit?"

I felt the blood drain from my face. My hands went numb. Was eleven years old too young for a heart attack? Well, if Red could have heart trouble as an infant, I guess I really could be about to explode.

"Of course it's in Detroit!" I shouted. My heart was pounding now, and I felt myself shaking.

Of course it was in Detroit. *Of course! Of course! Of course!*

Mom pulled herself up taller in her seat. She said, "Let's not freak out yet. I know this comes as a big shock. We've been here almost your whole lives. Brianna, you were born here, but we left briefly when I got a posting in Omaha. A year later, I was sent back here and we've made this our home. But..."

But?

No! No *but*! Detroit is home. I like home. This is home and I like it.

Katy reached over and patted Mom on the sleeve of her silky white blouse. She said, "Go on, Mom. But what?"

Now Mom looked from Katy to me and then at Dad. She turned toward him and placed one hand on his arm. I could almost feel his heart quicken under her touch. It might've been romantic if I wasn't afraid Mom was about to rip his heart out, too.

"David, you know I've grown to love it here. Detroit is our home. But when we came here and the girls were young, I made a conscious decision to take myself off the fast track. I wanted them to have roots. Normalcy. And they have. Now I've been with the bureau ten years and I'm being offered a supervisory position in Washington, D.C."

Daddy blew out a huge sigh. His head dropped down to his chest momentarily before looking back at all of us. No one's face was more expectant than Mom's.

The music began again, slow and deliberate. Bluesy with a lot of soul. A song with the same kind of sadness that yanked at your heart.

Mom, who almost never looked uncertain, bit her lip and leaned into Dad. She said, "You sacrificed your dream of becoming a doctor for my dream of becoming an FBI agent. Let me pay you back, David. With my raise, we could afford for you to attend a physician's assistant school, like we've discussed."

I wanted to shout, "NOOOOOOOOO!" But my tongue felt stuck.

"Baby, you don't owe me anything, so you don't need to pay anything back," he said. "We have a lot to discuss. But you know I'll support you. It's just... well, it's just a big shock. But I am so proud of you." He leaned in and kissed her cheek.

Mom smiled, then quickly looked at us girls again. "Don't worry, you two. If your father and I decide to take our family on this journey, it wouldn't be until June, after the person currently in that position retires. I'd have to go down a few times between now and then; otherwise I'll be here."

No one else was saying anything, so I said, "Mom, you can't be serious. I mean, I've been class president two years in a row. Blueberry Hills Middle needs me. And what about MY career? You know it'll be next to impossible to find another bakery like Wetzel's that'll let me bake and sell my goods."

"Honey, I know it would be difficult. Believe me. I did not come to this place lightly. But this whole raise and promotion thing was unexpected. Besides, you and your uncle Al got along so well in December, perhaps he'll let you set up shop in his restaurant."

She reached out and lightly placed her hand on my

wrist. "Sweetie, it's a high honor to be given an opportunity like this."

I pulled my wrist away. "Well, if you and your fabulous opportunity will excuse me," I said, "I have to go to the bathroom and throw up!"

I☆I☆I☆I

Needless to say, the ride home after that was kind of quiet. Except for suck-up Katy, who kept asking lame questions. "Ooo, Mom, what would your new job title be?" and "Mom, doesn't D.C. have excellent orchestras?" *Ugh!*

My face pressed hard against the icy cold window. Warm tears pushed past my eyelids. I needed to talk to my friends. But—and this shows how bad it was—I was too sad to text them.

We all trudged inside and began putting away our coats. Mom asked, "Brianna, how is your stomach?"

Despite several rinses, my mouth still tasted sour. I mentally scratched French toast cupcakes off my to-do list. I wouldn't be able to stand the smell of maple syrup for a year!

"It's okay," I barely whispered.

"Just in case, I'll get you something to settle your

tummy. I don't want you getting dehydrated," Mom said.

I was about to object when the doorbell stopped me in my tracks. Mom looked at Dad. He shrugged.

And I thought I didn't have a clue, either, until I twisted the knob, tugged on the oak door, and saw a person on our front porch.

My secret weapon!

After the way things fell apart at brunch, I forgot all about my surprise. Now here she stood, all dressed up in a black cashmere coat and cobalt-blue leather boots.

A sharp intake of air behind me. My mother. Then I felt her moving toward me, her hand on my shoulder.

I turned to say something, but before I could get the words out, she blurted:

"Mom! What on earth are you doing here?"

Reporter's Notebook

Sunday, January 14

To-Do List:

- One month to get ready for cheer exhibition
- Two weeks to finish journalism story
- SheCodes Event, 9:00 a.m. Saturday, January 27
- Three shifts at Wetzel's bakery this week!
- OPERATION ONLINE BAKERY starts today!!!

In coding, computer scientists or programmers write programs to solve problems and create more efficient ways of doing things. They also design new systems and machines, like robots, that rely on computers to operate.

I wonder if I could design my own Brianna Justice robot? My own Mini-Me!!!

12

"SURRR..." I started out loud and brightly, but one look at Mom and I finished with, "prise."

Grandmother Adeline Spencer, or Miss Addy, as I'd been calling her since I was a baby, was no ordinary granny. Probably why she didn't want anyone calling her Granny.

She was tall, especially in her rich blue stiletto boots. But she and Mom had the same shaped face. I guess that meant I did, too. She wore her hair long in loose locs that hung down her back and were golden brown, which looked good against her light, peachy skin. Her eyes were pale gray, almost blue, and her smile spread ear to ear.

"Brianna!" she said, rushing in and grabbing me in her arms. Over her shoulder, I saw Mom and Dad exchange confused looks. Katy stood back with her arms crossed over her chest. My heart started hammering like I'd done something really wrong, which of course, I certainly had not! I had just invited my dear, sweet grandmother to visit, that's all.

When Miss Addy finally released me, she took my face in her hands. "Little queen," she said. A simple statement. She was always telling me that all women are queens and powerful and should be encouraged to fly. Miss Addy was like that, kind of; you know, hippie-like.

Then she slowly turned me around and stepped aside.

"Jeannie? Oh, baby, please come and give your mama a hug," Miss Addy said.

"Mom, it's good to see you, but I'm just really surprised. What are you doing here?" my mother asked, hugging her.

Miss Addy turned and waggled her eyebrows at me. Then she said, "I was invited!"

Then she made the rounds, hugging everyone. Mom

asked, "Did you drive all the way down from Mackinac Island?"

Now Miss Addy was slipping off her coat and scarf, but still lugging a bunch of bags and packages. We all went into the living room and sat.

I sat real close to my grandmother while she explained. I suddenly felt like my knees might start knocking or my hands might shake. I linked my fingers with Miss Addy's while we sat on the sofa.

She went on talking in that warm, soothing tone she had, telling us how she'd locked up the inn and candy shop she'd owned for almost twenty years, and drove the seven hours from Michigan's Upper Peninsula.

"But why?" Mom said, sounding confused. Her gaze kept cutting from me back to Miss Addy. My leg trembled and my mouth was incredibly dry. This wasn't right. I had it all planned out.

1. We'd have a nice, relaxing brunch with Mom.
2. Next, we'd arrive home and I'd ask my parents to play a board game with us. They loved the whole family bonding thing.

3. Miss Addy would arrive.

4. She would come in and Mom would be so happy to see her mother. Then Miss Addy would help me convince Mom of all the reasons I should be able to have an online business.

Mom announcing she'd been offered a promotion, which meant she'd be able to boss around even more people, well, that was *NOT* part of my plan.

Is it in Detroit?

The question loomed over my thoughts like a cloud. At least Mom seemed happy to see Miss Addy, who was still trying to answer the "why" question, saying she and I had talked regularly since Christmas. She said she'd hated missing out for the holidays so she wanted to come now.

Then she produced the bags she'd brought in.

"Katy, this is for you," Miss Addy said, producing a long, slender box from one of the bags. "I know you play flute. I bought this one from an old friend of mine, an African American woman who is a famous flautist, Sherry Winston."

Katy's eyes went wide. She rushed over and took the box. Slowly, she removed the case, then opened it to find a white flute that sparkled like a grand piano.

"Grandmother, Miss Addy, I don't know what to say," gushed Katy. "It's beautiful. Thank you!" She immediately started tinkering with keys and so forth and began playing it.

Flute music. Yay, that's what this awkward moment needs.

I rolled my eyes. Miss Addy pretended not to notice, saying to Katy, "Enjoy, my darling." Then she pulled out two smaller bags, passing them to Mom and Dad.

Dad removed a University of Michigan cap and a huge block of homemade fudge.

He rushed over and threw his arms around her. Dad, like Katy, could be a real suck-up. Dad kissed her cheek and said, "Thank you! Thank you!"

When he stepped away, I saw my mom holding something I didn't understand. It was a pipe. She was cradling it like it was made of fragile glass, but I could see that it was made of wood.

"It's Daddy's old pipe," Mom said.

"I was going through some things and found that. I knew you would want to have it. You can't possibly hold it and not think of him. Jean, I know he's proud of you." Miss Addy's face beamed. Mom had gone away somewhere inside her head. She held the pipe like a baby bird and raised it to her face and took a big long sniff. Then she looked at her mother with a dreamy little smile.

"It still smells like him," Mom whispered.

"I know, baby," said Miss Addy.

We were all caught in the dreaminess of the moment. The dreamy moment was broken when we heard the back door crash open and Grandpa come stomping in.

"That snow is getting terrible!" he grumbled. "Adeline! That you?"

Grandpa spotted Miss Addy as he was taking his boots off. She went over to him, avoiding puddles of melting ice on the wooden floor around him. Dad grinned at his dad.

"Come here, you old fox!" Miss Addy said, wrapping him in a warm embrace. As they walked to the living room Grandpa said to Miss Addy, "Girl, what you doing here?"

Her eyes got too bright, and her voice sounded like a Disney Princess's. "Well, you see, Brianna here invited me. She's such a little entrepreneur, you know. And, well, she's planning, hoping to have her own business..." she was saying as she reached the sofa, pulled out the final bag, and took out what she'd brought for me.

It was a collection of things any business owner would love. And fancy, too. No, not fancy. Professional. A leather-bound legal pad with my name embossed on the top. And she had created a logo with the name of my company beneath it—Cupcake Ninja, Inc. At least, that was what I'd told her I wanted the name to be.

She handed me an envelope and said, "Look inside. The name is official. I had it incorporated just for you!"

Miss Addy was talking as I read the paperwork inside the envelope. She was sounding so wonderful, but I knew my mother, and I could see the pep talk wasn't working.

Truly, I appreciated what Grandmother Miss Addy was trying to do, but when Mom was in investigation mode, sneaking past her was hopeless. No wonder the FBI wanted to promote her. That woman was a human lie detector. She had turned toward me with her laser eyes. You don't want to ever be the one getting stared down by her laser eyes. Trust me.

My head dropped. I sighed.

"Okay, Mom. It's like this," I said. When I finally raised my head and met her laser vision—yikes!

Omigoodness! I feel her eyes burning into my soul. HELP!

I drew another deep breath and went on.

"Mom, Dad, you know how much I've wanted to start an online baking business. Well . . .

"Well . . . I thought if Miss Addy was here she could, you know, help me make my case," I said.

Testing . . . testing . . . Is this thing on?

Then I started babbling uncontrollably. Once again, motor-mouthing and wishing to goodness I would just shut up.

"Mom, before you say anything. Please. Just listen. Wait!" I ran into the kitchen and grabbed my iPad. Quickly I swiped to the app where I kept my notes. Once upon a time I used my clipboard to keep up with my lists.

I came back into the living room, heart pounding, hands sweating. "Look, Mom, Dad," I said, thrusting my iPad at their faces.

Top Reasons Why I Should Have an Online Business:

1. **Kids who own their own businesses learn how to be innovative, which is very important to our economy.**
2. **Owning a business teaches kids to be better planners.**
3. **It teaches hard work and...**

"**BRIANNA DIANE JUSTICE!**" Gulp! Oh, no! Not the whole name!

Mom was practically vibrating as she yelled my name. I froze, heart doing a swift kick. Uh-oh. I'm dead. Brianna Justice, dead at two-fifty-eight on Sunday.

"Mom, okay, let me just say—"

"Enough!" In my whole entire life, I had never seen Mom so angry. I was standing between her and dad. Poor Miss Addy was across from us, her strange, pale eyes looking at me with sympathy.

"You have said quite enough, Miss Missy!"

Oh, no! Not Miss Missy. She only broke that one out when she was ready to send someone to prison. For real. There are convicts walking around right now who were once her Miss Missys. They did hard time, y'all.

"Jean, wait," Dad said, reaching out for my mom. But she batted aside his hand and took a wide sidestep away from him and me.

She said, "You have pulled a lot of stunts in your day, young lady, but this really takes the *cupcake*. How you could even think that bringing my mother here was going to change my mind about an issue we've already discussed...well, you don't know how wrong you are!"

Oh, I think I was getting a strong idea just how wrong I'd been.

But she wasn't finished.

"Did you ever, even once, stop to think that I, we, made that decision because it was what was best for you? Did you?"

I blew out a sigh. My dry mouth turned bitter tasting and the burning in my chest that started out as fear was turning into something hotter—anger. I wasn't the problem. She was the one trying to yank us all out of our real

137

lives and force us to move to Washington, D.C. She had a lot of nerve being mad at me.

So I said, "I know you might've *thought* you were doing what was best for me." Okay, look. Every kid, especially girls, knows that there is a tone you don't use with your mom. You just don't. Not unless you really want to yank her chain. Well, I used that tone. And oh boy did it work!

My mom got this wild-eyed expression, like a crazy ghost woman in a horror movie. She held up her hand and used her fingers to tick off point after point, going down her invisible list.

"One, I told you I believe you're stretching yourself too thin. You want to be in everything and you just can't. Trying to do too much is making you unfocused. You're all over the place! Two, I told you your dad and I thought spending so much time at the bakery was keeping you from just being a kid. And three, no one ever said you could *never* have an online business. We said you couldn't have one NOW! You act like eleven is at the edge of retirement. You can't wait until you're fourteen, in high school, to have your own business?

"Mom, what's the difference? I proved I could be

responsible enough to work in the bakery, save my money, keep my grades up, and make new friends. All the things you said you wanted for me, wanted *from* me. I did it, and it's like I'm getting punished anyway!"

Katy, my perfect and tranquil big sister who never seemed to disappoint my mother, stepped forward. *Here it comes*, I thought. She was going to take this opportunity to really make me look bad.

"Mom, I'm sure Brianna didn't mean any harm. You know how she gets carried away. She's just always so excited about her money," she said. I felt my mouth fall open, shocked that Katy was defending me when she could've tried to bury me.

But Mom wasn't having it.

"Thank you, Katy, for playing peacemaker, but this time she has gone too far." Mom turned to me again and said, "Brianna, you need to go to your room. And don't you even think about coming out. I don't want to even look at you right now."

Great! I'm in federal lockdown. Will I have to make a lock pick out of soap and break out? I half expected her to cuff me. I spun around to say something, but she shut me down.

"You have the right to remain silent. Girl, you better use it!"

I couldn't help it. I gave her such a dirty look that I scared myself. Then I stomped loudly up each step while releasing the anguished cry of frustration only an innovative eleven-year-old can understand:

"Grrrrrrrnghhhh!"

And in the language of kids all over the world, I used the only weapon available. This is for all the kids unfairly bossed around by their parents. All the kids who've been misunderstood and confined without a proper trial. WHERE IS MY DUE PROCESS?

Taking glorious aim, and using every aching muscle in my body:

Yes, I slammed my bedroom door.

Take that, *Mom*!

Reporter's Notebook

"When I talk to girls about the future, I like to ask: 'When you leave this earth, whose life do you want to have made better? What do you want to be better on this earth because you were here?'

"When you put it on a very practical level I think girls look at the question differently and understand they are or can be part of that discussion."

—Dr. Quincy Brown, PhD Program Director, STEM Education Research American Association for the Advancement of Science (AAAS)

13

The next day was Dr. Martin Luther King Jr.'s holiday. No school.

Thank goodness at the last minute Toya invited me and Red over to spend the night. Apparently, my mom had been too outraged to ground me. When Toya's mom called her, I'd overheard her on the phone saying, "Please, Carrie, come and get her. I haven't been home four hours and already I need a break from Miss Mouth!"

Well! I wasn't exactly celebrating her return, either.

"*Omigod!* Justice, what did you do?" both Red and Toya asked. When I explained, they stared at me openmouthed.

Toya was the first to speak. She said, "Girl, you're

nodded. "Well, living in Texas, we didn't always have the most enlightened folks in our community. I never understood how grown people could be so afraid of people they didn't know or refused to meet. I'm glad my parents were never like that. They always encouraged me to have all kinds of friends. But a lot of kids I knew did not have it that way. There is a lot of ignorance in the world."

We got to talking about the story Red and I were working on. Neither of us told Toya about the conversation at the gym. Perhaps we were both too embarrassed to bring it up.

However, we did talk about neighborhoods and being disadvantaged and stuff like that. It wasn't long before the smell of warm, baked chocolate cupcakes, filled with chocolate morsels and topped with homemade caramel and buttery baked pecans and cream cheese frosting, filled the entire world.

Steamed windows hid the frosty beyond. We were cleaning up when her mom came home. We all held our breath for a second. I already had one mother mad at me, I didn't need another. But she grinned and immediately snatched up a cupcake and bit into it.

"Oh, baby, that's heaven!" she exclaimed.

When it was time to go, we changed out of our pj's and gathered our things. Toya surprised me by giving me a DVD.

"It's called *A Raisin in the Sun*, by Lorraine Hansberry. You should watch it when you have a chance. Might give you some ideas for your story."

I said I would, then Red and I piled into her mother's car. We sat side by-side in the back seat. What we'd been avoiding all night and day sat between us like a big, funky elephant.

Finally, I turned to her and said, "I'm not moving. I can't. I won't," I whispered.

When she turned to me, her blue eyes were watery, but the smile at the corners of her lips curled up. She said, "Yes, you will. I didn't want to leave Texas, either. But look at us. You'll make new friends. I'll be on the cheer team and hopefully will make more friends." She shrugged. "That's how it works with friends and families."

I sighed deep into my soul, wanting so much for everything she said *not* to be true.

Reporter's Notebook

Tuesday, January 16

"What happens to a dream deferred?
Does it dry up like a raisin in the sun?"
   —Langston Hughes (1951)

Lorraine Hansberry was the first African American to have a play on Broadway, *A Raisin in the Sun*. Her award-winning play, whose title comes from the famous poem "Harlem," by Langston Hughes, debuted on Broadway in 1959. *A Raisin in the Sun* is about a black family trying to leave a poor neighborhood in Chicago to live somewhere cleaner, safer, and more beautiful—a place where the white residents don't want them to be.

At the *Free Press*, Red, McSweater Vest, and I were hard at work going over our notes and planning our strategy. I knew it wasn't the same as investigating scammers or other crooks on TV news, but I was getting excited.

I said, "I just want my story—"

Red cleared her throat.

"Sorry. Our story to really help others. Maybe it can have the impact of helping folks over there get jobs or at least better access to things like technology in schools."

McSweater Vest grinned, then raised his hands in a calm-down gesture. He said, "Whoa! Love the enthusiasm, but realistically there is only so much one story can do. However, it is good to discuss your story goal. What else would you girls like to happen as a result of your work?"

Red and I exchanged glances. She did a half shrug and said, "I guess I never thought about that. I'm not sure."

But I said, "Well, I have thought about it a lot. Disadvantaged kids shouldn't have to live in neighborhoods like that—glass broken all over the streets; doors with bars on them; I want my...uh, *our* story to make people take notice. Take action. Clean up the east side and make it a better place to live!"

A booming laugh came from behind McSweater Vest. Buffalo Bob, once again driving his rolling chair, came into view.

"So, you think you can fix all the woes over there, one of the most economically strapped neighborhoods, with one story in the *Freep*?" He threw his large head back and let out another gust of laughter. Today's T-shirt read:

"NOTHING IN THE WORLD IS MORE DANGEROUS THAN SINCERE IGNORANCE AND CONSCIENTIOUS STUPIDITY."

—*DR. MARTIN LUTHER KING JR.*

"Hey, Bob," McSweater Vest greeted his colleague. I did an eye roll. I had learned that good ol' Buffalo Bob had a lot of ideas and he wasn't shy at all about expressing them.

"Nice shirt," I said. He gave a snort.

"Who's the new recruit?" he asked, nodding toward Red. We got them introduced. Bob said his hellos, and then turned his attention back to me.

"Couldn't help overhearing your little speech about Detroit's east side. I couldn't tell if you were planning a journalism story or running for office," he said.

"She is president of the WHOLE sixth grade," Red drawled.

I threw her an eye roll, as well. Pretty soon I'd be past my daily limit. I said, "Excuse me, but what's wrong with wanting to do something that will lead to change and improvement?"

I'd been thinking a lot about what happened at Price. Talking to Toya had reminded me I did know who I was. I was someone who took action. If something's broken, you fix it, right?

So if you don't want to be made fun of for where you live, then you've got to get out of there or stop living that lifestyle. Right? I wouldn't like being thought of as ghetto. That neighborhood didn't look so bad, but everyone talked about wanting to get out. I don't understand why, if crime is the problem, can't they just get rid of the bad people? Right? RIGHT?

I'm wiped out. I think your mom is right. You're trying to do too much. But that's just my opinion," she said.

I nodded, but wasn't a hundred percent convinced. My mind was constantly working. I was always thinking about what I wanted to do or be or how to achieve something.

Red stared at me like she was reading my thoughts. She drawled, "Whatch'all need is to learn how to unplug. You know, sit quietly and meditate or do yoga or something."

I gave her such a hard look. Yoga! Oh, brother!

We decided to forget about my problems for a while and just have fun.

Still in our pj's after lunch, we took bowls of popcorn into the den and vegged out watching movies. I was having such a good time that I didn't want to think much about Mom and our blowup. Not to mention how ashamed I'd been of myself after what happened at the gym.

"Toya." I turned to my friend. "Do you ever watch those memes or videos that talk about people who act ghetto?"

She snorted. "Not if I want to live. My mom would

trying to start your own business now, too. On top of everything else?"

"You're moving?" Red asked in a hoarse whisper.

I couldn't even look at Red because my eyes were watering from trying not to think about it.

So I said to Toya, "I really think I can handle it."

Toya didn't go to Blueberry Hills Middle. She lived out in Bloomfield Hills and went to private school. Her father was a big-time attorney. I wondered if he'd represent me—Brianna Justice vs. Mom's *in*Justice.

She was tall, African American, with a beautiful tiny Afro and great smile. I couldn't get over how much her hair had grown in just a few months. I'd met her when I'd written a story for the *Blueberry* about how she and another friend of hers had shaved their heads to match a third friend's, Lacy, when Lacy lost her hair to chemotherapy. After the story, Toya and I hung out and now we were really good friends. What I liked most about her was that she was a tell-it-like-it-is friend.

"I take piano lessons and Mandarin Chinese because Dad is convinced that one day China will rule the world. He says when that happens, I need to speak the language. But just those two things a week, plus regular stuff, and go!" She jumped up and we followed. Their kitchen was amazing. I dug out pots and pans; flour, sugar, eggs, oil. I decided to do the same cupcake I'd done for Wetzel's last week. I groaned a little, remembering that bright and early—five in the morning—I had to be up and at the bakery before going to school.

Deep sigh. No time to get cranky about it now. Instead, we found chocolate morsels, butter, and cream. "It's the recipe for my 'I Have a Dream' cupcakes in celebration of Dr. Martin Luther King Jr."

Red asked, "Why do you always call him the doctor and junior part when you say his name? Why not just Martin Luther King?"

Toya looked at me. I was elbow-deep in my batter but had to laugh. Before I could answer, Toya jumped in.

"Because he worked hard for that doctorate and when we remember him, we have to remember his struggle to get it," she said.

I nodded. "And because if we don't honor him as such, it gives power to those who worked so hard to tear him down. At least, that's what Grandpa always says when I forget to call him Dr. King."

I glanced at Red to see if that offended her, but she

go ballistic and Dad would be signing me up for African
dance classes *again*!"

When I looked at her, she shrugged, and said, "When
you live in the suburbs with predominantly white people,
like out here, your parents get real sensitive if they think
you're forgetting your black roots." By "out here," she was
talking about Bloomfield Hills, a very wealthy suburb of
Detroit that was considered mostly white. No big deal to
me, but I understood exactly what Toya meant.

"Do you ever feel like you're forgetting your roots?"
I asked.

"Heck no!" Her answer was matter-of-fact. "No matter
where I live, I know where I come from. I am the proud
descendant of slaves. Daddy used to be into that whole
trace your roots thing. I know when his ancestors were
brought to America and everything. I know who I am."

I flipped onto my back.

I knew who I was, too. At least, I thought I did. Dad
and Mom hadn't traced their ancestry, but I just figured
we came from wherever all black Americans come from.

"Hey, do you think your mom would mind if we
baked something?" I asked suddenly.

Toya's face lit up. "If she does, I don't care. Let's

nodded. "Well, living in Texas, we didn't always have the most enlightened folks in our community. I never understood how grown people could be so afraid of people they didn't know or refused to meet. I'm glad my parents were never like that. They always encouraged me to have all kinds of friends. But a lot of kids I knew did not have it that way. There is a lot of ignorance in the world."

We got to talking about the story Red and I were working on. Neither of us told Toya about the conversation at the gym. Perhaps we were both too embarrassed to bring it up.

However, we did talk about neighborhoods and being disadvantaged and stuff like that. It wasn't long before the smell of warm, baked chocolate cupcakes, filled with chocolate morsels and topped with homemade caramel and buttery baked pecans and cream cheese frosting, filled the entire world.

Steamed windows hid the frosty beyond. We were cleaning up when her mom came home. We all held our breath for a second. I already had one mother mad at me, I didn't need another. But she grinned and immediately snatched up a cupcake and bit into it.

"Oh, baby, that's heaven!" she exclaimed.

147

When it was time to go, we changed out of our pj's and gathered our things. Toya surprised me by giving me a DVD.

"It's called *A Raisin in the Sun*, by Lorraine Hansberry. You should watch it when you have a chance. Might give you some ideas for your story."

I said I would, then Red and I piled into her mother's car. We sat side by-side in the back seat. What we'd been avoiding all night and day sat between us like a big, funky elephant.

Finally, I turned to her and said, "I'm not moving. I can't. I won't," I whispered.

When she turned to me, her blue eyes were watery, but the smile at the corners of her lips curled up. She said, "Yes, you will. I didn't want to leave Texas, either. But look at us. You'll make new friends. I'll be on the cheer team and hopefully will make more friends." She shrugged. "That's how it works with friends and families."

I sighed deep into my soul, wanting so much for everything she said *not* to be true.

Reporter's Notebook

"What happens to a dream deferred?
Does it dry up like a raisin in the sun?"
—Langston Hughes (1951)

Lorraine Hansberry was the first African American to have a play on Broadway, *A Raisin in the Sun*. Her award-winning play, whose title comes from the famous poem "Harlem," by Langston Hughes, debuted on Broadway in 1959. *A Raisin in the Sun* is about a black family trying to leave a poor neighborhood in Chicago to live somewhere cleaner, safer, and more beautiful—a place where the white residents don't want them to be.

14

At the *Free Press*, Red, McSweater Vest, and I were hard at work going over our notes and planning our strategy. I knew it wasn't the same as investigating scammers or other crooks on TV news, but I was getting excited.

I said, "I just want my story—"

Red cleared her throat.

"Sorry. Our story to really help others. Maybe it can have the impact of helping folks over there get jobs or at least better access to things like technology in schools."

McSweater Vest grinned, then raised his hands in a calm-down gesture. He said, "Whoa! Love the enthusiasm, but realistically there is only so much one story can do. However, it is good to discuss your story goal. What else would you girls like to happen as a result of your work?"

Red and I exchanged glances. She did a half shrug and said, "I guess I never thought about that. I'm not sure."

But I said, "Well, I have thought about it a lot. Disadvantaged kids shouldn't have to live in neighborhoods like that—glass broken all over the streets; doors with bars on them; I want my...uh, *our* story to make people take notice. Take action. Clean up the east side and make it a better place to live!"

A booming laugh came from behind McSweater Vest. Buffalo Bob, once again driving his rolling chair, came into view.

"So, you think you can fix all the woes over there, one of the most economically strapped neighborhoods, with one story in the *Freep*?" He threw his large head back and let out another gust of laughter. Today's T-shirt read:

"NOTHING IN THE WORLD IS MORE DANGEROUS THAN SINCERE IGNORANCE AND CONSCIENTIOUS STUPIDITY."

—*DR. MARTIN LUTHER KING JR.*

"Hey, Bob," McSweater Vest greeted his colleague. I did an eye roll. I had learned that good ol' Buffalo Bob had a lot of ideas and he wasn't shy at all about expressing them.

"Nice shirt," I said. He gave a snort.

"Who's the new recruit?" he asked, nodding toward Red. We got them introduced. Bob said his hellos, and then turned his attention back to me.

"Couldn't help overhearing your little speech about Detroit's east side. I couldn't tell if you were planning a journalism story or running for office," he said.

"She is president of the WHOLE sixth grade," Red drawled.

I threw her an eye roll, as well. Pretty soon I'd be past my daily limit. I said, "Excuse me, but what's wrong with wanting to do something that will lead to change and improvement?"

I'd been thinking a lot about what happened at Price. Talking to Toya had reminded me I did know who I was. I was someone who took action. If something's broken, you fix it, right?

So if you don't want to be made fun of for where you live, then you've got to get out of there or stop living that lifestyle. Right? I wouldn't like being thought of as ghetto. That neighborhood didn't look so bad, but everyone talked about wanting to get out. I don't understand why, if crime is the problem, can't they just get rid of the bad people? Right? RIGHT?

right but you suddenly think you might not be. Venus, that girl from Price, her face popped into my mind.

Buffalo Bob hefted himself from his seat.

Still scowling, he went to a computer terminal, bent down, then decided he needed to sit again. His fingers flew across the keys. He tapped a few more keystrokes, then pushed back.

Pointing at the screen, he said, "Read!"

I could feel Red behind me, reading, too. When we finished, my eyes had filled with tears and my lips trembled. I felt foolish and confused.

"I'll bet you thought that word had something to do with black people, didn't you?" Buffalo Bob asked, though now his tone was gentler.

All I could do was nod. All the videos and memes and jokes and everything about being ghetto always showed black or brown people living a certain way. But that wasn't what the short article said.

Buffalo Bob nodded at the screen. "My wife wrote that," he said. "She's Jewish. Her great-grandparents died in Nazi death camps during World War II. When we did one of those DNA tests to trace our heritage, hers went all the way back to Venice in the 1500s."

According to the article, the term *ghetto* was first used by Venetians. They forced all Jews to live in a separate section of the city. Then they built walls around it and would lock them in. The doors opened twice a day. To let people out for work and then let them back in.

Finally, throat dry and eyes leaking, I asked, "But why?"

"Short answer," said McSweater Vest. "Ignorance. Even before the 1500s, back as far as the 1100s, a part of the Catholic Church decided Christians and Jews should not be allowed to live together. So segregation became the law."

Buffalo Bob nodded. "But it took our friends the Venetians to give that practice a name," he said. "When the living conditions got too crowded, the Jews had to build their living quarters higher and higher because with the walls around them, that was the only way they could expand."

"I always thought Venice was a lovely place," whispered Red. "I've always wanted to visit and ride boats along the canals."

Now Buffalo Bob smiled, looking like his old self. "I've been to Venice with my wife. You should go. It is a lovely city—now. What happened there became the

156

law all over Europe. It wasn't just the Venetians. And in Germany, during World War II, Jews were once again confined to horrific living conditions!"

McSweater Vest must have seen the look of disgust and complete shock on my face. He placed a hand on my shoulder and said, "Now, now. We've gotten slightly off track, Brianna."

But a stern expression in Buffalo Bob's eyes held my gaze. He leaned forward, placing his meaty palm on my hand.

"Imagine, Brianna, the filthy, wretched living conditions Jews had to endure. That was the law all over Europe for centuries. The histories of immigrants worldwide are riddled with stories of ghettos—sections reserved for the poor, the disadvantaged."

I gulped. Numbness tingled on my lips like I'd eaten way too many hot wings.

My mind raced back to the gym. Lori and Sandra Poe. The way they were quick to point out that me and Tracy weren't like the others.

Ghetto.

Black girls.

Ghetto girls.

An image of the "Go Ask Darnell" character popped into my head. The boy who took so much delight in imitating what he considered to be girls in the ghetto. Harmless, I'd thought.

If you don't want to be called ghetto, then don't act ghetto.

My mantra.

Queasiness slipped around inside my belly, making me feel ready to throw up.

Buffalo Bob continued, "Girls, this is important to you as reporters because you need to know context. You need to understand that certain words and phrases are far more powerful and damaging than you think. And you need to understand that the mentality that created poor neighborhoods didn't start in Detroit. Or with black people. It's been going strong for centuries and it's worldwide."

"So does this mean the people on the east side are being made to live there?" I asked. Not because they were black, I knew. Because I was black and my neighborhood did not look like that.

Another woman joined us. She pulled up a seat. I hadn't realized it, but we were in sort of a semicircle. Red had moved her chair to sit beside me and slipped her thin hand under the armrest of the office chair. We entwined our fingers. I felt grateful for her support.

"I'm eavesdropping," the woman said. "My name is Joy Stein."

"A proud Jewish woman," Buffalo Bob proclaimed with a wink.

"Yeah, yeah, yeah," she said. "Look, girls, I did overhear your conversation. Can't help it. McShea and I share a cubicle wall. To answer your question, no, the people over there aren't necessarily there because they're black. Over time, the word *ghetto* was used to classify any urban area that had pockets of poor people. When whole groups get discriminated against, however, they are bound to suffer more," she said.

"Let's face it, a lot of immigrants who came to this country were poor. None were poorer than the Africans after slavery was abolished. I've been fighting this same battle with my twelve-year-old daughter. 'Ghetto' this and 'ghetto' that. Now it's used as a means of making fun of people. But almost always, it's aimed at people of color. My own daughter didn't know the origin of the word until I couldn't take it anymore and talked to her about it," she added.

Buffalo Bob took over again.

He said, "Look, none of this has anything to do with the story you're writing. What it does affect is the attitude you have as you're writing it. Language is a powerful tool. Choose your words wisely!"

After that, Buffalo Bob and Joy Stein stayed and helped us devise a story strategy. McSweater Vest told us that discrimination in America had been a way of life, forcing many African Americans into certain sections of the city. He said President Lyndon B. Johnson signed the Fair Housing Act of 1968, making it illegal to keep someone from buying or renting based on race, sex, or anything else, other than money.

I was writing notes furiously by the end, trying to take it all in. Miss Joy ran to her desk before we left and came back with a book.

The Jungle, by Upton Sinclair.

"1906!" I said when I opened the cover and looked at the publication date.

Buffalo Bob fixed his face with a playful scowl. Trust me, after that beat-down I just got, I knew the difference now. He said, "Although it's called a fictional version of his investigation, Mr. Sinclair's book led to major changes in how our country inspects and handles our meat products. By the way, if you're squeamish, you might want to skip over some parts." He grimaced. All the adults did the same.

I☆I☆I☆I

Later, unable to sleep, I dug around and found the DVD Toya had given me. At first, it was a trip watching the old movie that was once an award-winning play. The story made me think about life—my life—even though it was from such a long time ago.

By the time I drifted off to sleep, Lorraine Hansberry and her play had given me an idea.

I had a big favor to ask Mrs. G., too. Not only did I have an idea for the *Blueberry*, I also knew what I wanted to do for Presidents' Day.

This time, it wasn't about making myself a better reporter, but hopefully sharing important new ideas with my fellow students!

Now all I had to do was figure out how to end the deep freeze with Mom.

Reporter's Notebook

Thursday, January 18

"You're not to be so blind with
patriotism that you can't face real-
ity. Wrong is wrong, no matter who
does it or says it."

—Malcolm X

So tired!!!

(MOM MUST NEVER KNOW!!!)

15

McSweater Vest called and said several girls at Price had invited me and Red to come back. We picked Thursday after school. However, Red had an unexpected appointment and couldn't go. It was decided that I could go if I wanted to. My mentor said he had stuff to do and I could hang out with Miss Newsome.

When it came time to return to Price Academy, Buffalo Bob's smack-down to my emotions still tingled in my brain.

But when we arrived, Shania, Shakira, and Venus said that if I wanted to get an inside look at "how it goes down" at Price, I should go to the basketball game with them. It was in the school's gym. Shakira and Venus were also on the cheer squad.

"You can ask us questions during the game," Shakira said.

"Ask me anything!" Shania said with a wide grin.

So, what could I say?

With so much going on, I didn't have time to freak out about seeing the kids at Price again.

I was surprised to see so many kids stay after school for the game. When Shania asked if our school had basketball games, I said, "Yeah, but they're lucky if a few dozen kids stay after. This gym is packed."

"Basketball season is, like, a big deal out here," Shania said. "Even for the middle school. Everybody comes out. Gotta represent!"

Still holding on to my notebook, I followed her into the stands. We sat a few rows up from the cheerleaders. The band was playing. Kids were dancing. The cold from outside was swallowed by the steamy heat of bodies wrapped in winter wear filling up the space.

How in the world was I supposed to conduct an interview in here?

A whistle blew and I realized the game had begun. Boys ran up and down the court. Price Academy was the Panthers; their opponents, the Eagles. At first, I was so confused about what to do.

However, it wasn't long before I was totally into it. Shakira smiled a lot while she cheered. Venus was a lot sassier, shaking her hips and shouting loud and proud to the beat of the band's music.

Back and forth the boys raced. I felt a longing to shout, "Pass me the rock!" That was what Daddy called a basketball. It had been more than a year since I'd played for a team. Until now, I hadn't thought much about it.

Hmm...maybe I could add basketball to my list of activities next year.

Thinking about next year made me cringe. Next year I would be in D.C. Before I could agonize over it, I got jostled and shaken out of my thoughts. I looked over to see that Alicia had joined us, sitting on the other side of Shania. When I looked at her, I think she growled at me. Oh, well.

It was interesting watching the cheerleaders. Competitive cheer was all about precision. Timing. Accuracy. But the Price Panther cheerleaders were all about getting the crowd pumped with attitude, energy, and fun dance moves.

When a time-out came, the cheerleaders raced onto

the floor, got into formation, and did a cheer the crowd must've been waiting for. "Roar, Panthers, roar!" All hips and shoulders and smiles. A few flips and two splits. *Boom!* The crowd was on its feet. It was electrifying.

They raced back to the sideline and Shakira leaned into the stands, high-fiving Shania but looking at me. She said, beaming, "That's our favorite routine. I know we might not be as fancy as your team, but tell the truth. We've got more soul, right?"

I gave her a look. She laughed, not a mean laugh, just what I was coming to understand was a Shakira laugh. "Girl, it don't matter. Y'all might get to travel and compete and all that, but we're here, doing our *thang*!"

Shakira danced her way back to her cheer line and Shania leaned over. "Shakira just playing," she said. "We're teasing you because you live way out in Orchard Park and not on the east side. It's all good."

I wanted to understand what she meant. My neighborhood was only thirty-five or so minutes away. It's not like I lived out in Toya's neighborhood. Now, that was fancy.

"Shania, it's not like I live in Bloomfield Hills. Orchard Park is far from fancy!"

That earned me another glare-growl combo. Alicia

leaned forward, shoulders hunched, mumbling to herself, "Yeah, Orchard Park might as well be Bloomfield Hills!"

Shania looked at Alicia, then at me. I started to say something, but the embarrassed look on Shania's face made me turn away instead.

Pretty soon halftime came. I tried talking to Shania about SheCodes, but of course, that didn't go anywhere because people were talking, laughing, and dancing. The Panthers were leading the game and everybody was feeling good. Instead of the band, music blared from overhead speakers.

I was standing, looking around the gym, watching all the chaos, when I felt a little tap on my shoulder. I turned around to find McSweater Vest.

"Hey, how's it going?" he asked.

"Okay, I guess." I shouted to be heard. He pointed to the bleachers and we sat.

He said, "Interviews not going so well?"

"Not going at all!" I admitted. "I mean, I'm having a good time. These games are nothing like at my school. So many people. Parents. High school kids. This place is packed."

His response surprised me. "Why do you think that is?"

I looked at him. Shrugged. "I don't know."

"You know, understanding this crowd might go a long way toward helping you understand why SheCodes is such an important event for this community," he said.

Huh?

"I don't understand."

"Look around," he said. "Think about your story. What are you and Red writing about?"

"We're writing about a program that will teach computer coding to minority girls, especially girls from disadvantaged neighborhoods," I answered.

"And what else?"

My heart did a high kick. What else? WHAT ELSE? There was no "what else." I felt caught off guard and confused. Two emotions I really, really HATED.

But McSweater Vest smiled. "Think about it, Brianna. Aside from being a way to educate the girls on computer science, what else will a day-long festival with a bunch of young girls, professional women, and activities provide?"

I was quiet for a long moment. I really did feel thrown off. Finally, in more of a question than a statement, I said, "It's something to do?"

He grinned. "Precisely! Part of being disadvantaged means a lack of access to positive experiences with your kids. Come on, let's go talk to some people."

Before I could protest, there he went, bow tie, sweater vest, and all. Marching toward a cluster of parents laughing it up.

"Excuse us," McSweater Vest said. He waited for me, and when I held back, he reached out and pulled me closer.

He introduced us to a group of adults who were staring at us in open curiosity.

But when he told them who we were and that I was writing a story for the *Freep* about their kids, one woman cut in and asked, "You're not writing one of them stories about how bad our kids are, are you?"

"No ma'am," I said. "I'm, well, me and my friend Red, our story is about the computer training programming coming up at the Lakeside Sports Complex. SheCodes." Her suspicious expression transformed into a grin. All of the parents were bobbing their heads.

The woman who'd spoken first said, "My grandbaby is going to that program," she said. "I think it's an excellent opportunity."

Now McSweater Vest was beaming, too. He said to the parents, "My young reporter here was wondering why this basketball game is so well attended. I thought if she talked to some folks, she might be able to incorporate it into her story."

Now he was grinning, the parents and grandparents were bobbing their heads in agreement, but I still didn't quite understand the connection.

This time it was one of the men who spoke. He said his name was Tyrus Diggs. "These games are something positive for the kids. They don't cost much money. The school does a good job of not letting teenagers from rival schools in here. You have to show your school ID to get into the door. It's safe, unless the boys on the team throw a haymaker at somebody because of a foul or something. And that kind of foolish behavior has almost disappeared since the new principal came."

The first woman, Maybel Brown, spoke up. "We don't have a lot of opportunities over here for the kids, so a lot of 'em end up hanging out and getting into trouble," Ms. Brown said.

Shirley Stewart, the mother of three boys and a daughter between the ages of four and fourteen, said it was hard keeping kids cooped up in the house just because you were trying to keep them safe. "When you can get them out of the house to enjoy fun with other kids, you do it."

I was writing fast, trying to keep up with them. When I looked up, finally, I asked:

"What about things like going to the library or the movies?"

Several of them snorted with laughter. Mr. Diggs asked, "Where you live, girlie?" He didn't sound mean or mad like Alicia. Just curious.

I told him I lived in Orchard Park. He said their neighborhood didn't have a movie theater or a library. "A lot of the parents you see here work real early or real late—that's how we can be here in the middle of the afternoon. Still, it's a lot of folks who are working long hours. Some work two jobs. So they can't be here.

"It's not like out there where you live. Orchard Park is a pretty area. I used to have a house in Orchard Park when my kids were little. But when the economy tanked, I got laid off at General Motors. I filed bankruptcy. Lost my house." He shrugged. The others were nodding their agreement.

Miss Stewart said, "It happens. One minute you're

going along fine, the next thing you know, wham! Life pulls the rug out from under you. Then you're struggling to get by day to day. Bringing my kids to these games, getting out with them as much as possible, it's my way of showing them that I love them. I want them to stay positive and when the time is right, make better choices than I did at their age."

Now it was McSweater Vest's turn to jump in.

"Who here is taking a child to the computer coding event?"

"Oh, I'll be there bright and early," said Ms. Brown. "My granddaughter is looking forward to it. And since they have sessions for parents, too, I can't wait. I never had something like that when I was in school. I want my baby to learn that there's more to life than just getting by. I want her to know she can succeed at anything!"

We talked a little longer, then the buzzer blared, signaling the start of the second half. I went back to where I'd been sitting with Shania. She had returned from the concession stand.

When we all sat down, I wound up between her and Alicia. I could actually feel the dislike oozing from Alicia and into me. Finally, I turned to her and asked:

"What's up, Alicia? What is the deal? Why're you hating on me?" The question seemed to catch her off guard. She grumped, looked down at her feet, then finally looked up.

"You must look at us, our neighborhood, our school, and think we're like a bad movie on cable. We're not all like the stereotypes, you know?" It was like she wanted to be angry, but halfway into her little speech, she lost steam—went from aggressive to just plain sad.

Then, before I could say anything, she asked, "What do your parents do for a living? Where do they work?"

"My dad is a nurse at Orchard Park Regional and my mother is a supervisor with the FBI."

That made her sit back, eyes wide. "Your mom is in the FBI? As in, the Law. The Man. The Fuzz."

"Um, yeah."

Something about her expression made us both burst out laughing. I'd never, ever thought of my mom as "The Man"!

We went back to watching the game. I hunched over my lap to write my notes.

I was beginning to see McSweater Vest's point. Something like SheCodes was about more than computer training. Simply holding the event in this neighborhood was cause for excitement.

The mood in the hallway was happy and light as we waited outside the gym. The Panthers had won and the crowd was mellow. I stood chatting with several of the cheerleaders, plus Shania and Alicia. The cheer girls wanted to ask me questions about the competitive cheer squad.

"That junk is expensive," said a cheerleader named Davlon Dean. "I know your mama and daddy must be rich."

"We're not rich," I countered, thinking back to how easily Dad had written the check for his portion. "I work in a bakery. The owner lets me sell my own cupcakes. I have money saved up."

"You paid for it with your cupcake money?" Davlon asked.

"Well, no," I admitted.

Alicia grumbled, "At the bakery, is the owner lady white? Does she treat you like you're trying to steal from her store?"

That made me laugh. "No! Why would she?" I asked, thinking she was joking.

The rest of the girls laughed, too. But Shakira said, "See, if it was one of us girls from the east side working at a bakery over here, I bet the store owner would make us walk through an X-ray machine like they do at the airport!" She sniggered out a laugh.

"Or at least wave an electronic wand over us," added Venus.

It was like they were joking, laughing at the idea. Yet, their tones had hard edges, their eyes cloudy with anger over the idea of being scanned or swept with an electronic wand.

Venus looked at me and said, "You're so lucky and I bet you don't even know it. Do your parents take part of your money to pay for stuff?"

"What stuff?" I asked.

She went googly-eyed. "What stuff? Stuff like rent, electricity, or groceries. When I babysit, I always give most of my money to my mom."

I frowned. It had never occurred to me to give my cupcake money to my parents.

Venus shook her head. "See, you're just spoiled. Do you have a maid to clean your room? Do you have chores?"

It sank in that they'd surrounded me, sort of. Enclosed

me in a circle of suspicion and doubt. It was my turn to shake my head.

"No, we don't have a maid. Well, not a regular one. Sometimes when Mom has been working out of town and Daddy has long hours at the hospital they'll arrange for a cleaner to come; otherwise me and my sister do the housework."

Another round of sniggering, like what I'd said was the most ridiculous thing ever.

Another girl asked:

"If your parents are rich enough for you to live in Orchard Park, why you out hustling cupcakes, anyway?"

"I'm not hustling cupcakes," I shot back. "I love to bake."

Then Alicia looked me up and down. From the tips of my black leather Air Jordans, to my black designer jeans, to the neat button-up cardigan and white shirt, to the exquisitely upright bun on my head.

Alicia said, "I'm not hating on you or nothing, but little black girls living in the suburbs with black skin on the outside but talking like white girls are frontin'. You want to be black, but you're not really. No offense, but you're an Oreo. Black on the outside, but all creamy and white in the middle."

My mouth dropped open. *What the what?* How could anyone make the beautiful delicious treat that is an Oreo cookie sound like something evil?

By the time my lips stopped sputtering and the pinpricks of anger stopped tickling my cheeks, they were already laughing. Shakira said, "Don't feel bad. It's not your fault you sound all proper like a white girl. Miss Newsome calls it the King's English. I bet that's just how everybody sound where you live."

Shania and Venus nodded in agreement. I shook my head.

"I'm black just like all of you," I said, hating myself for sounding weak and uncertain. Alicia cut her eyes to me like she could smell my confusion.

"Black folks over here are nothing like you. You're like a visitor from another planet. One who looks like us," she said in a deadly serious way, "but really, on the inside, we're nothing alike."

"A visitor from Planet Oreo!" someone said, and they all burst into laughter—at my expense—Shania saying, "Girl, don't pay us no mind. You're cool and all, just..."

Her unspoken words hung in the air like a misguided

cheerleader—the flying kind. You're cool and all . . . just not as cool as us!

When I'd overheard those boys in the hall on my first visit, all I wanted to do was set myself apart and make them understand how different I was. Now? A knot tightened in my chest.

Coming here today was supposed to bring us closer together. Show them that I wasn't afraid and didn't want to stereotype them; I'd learned my lesson. Now it seemed they were the ones stereotyping me. Big-time!

On the car ride back with McSweater Vest, I seethed over the girls' comments. Earlier in the month, discovering spilled Oreo packages in the snow had felt like a gift from up above. Who didn't love Oreos?

But being called one by a bunch of girls who were questioning my blackness all because of where I lived, how I spoke, and what my family did for a living was no gift.

Planet Oreo? *Girl, bye!*

Getting stereotyped sucked.

I had a notebook full of quotes and conversations, but I realized, I still didn't have enough answers!

Reporter's Notebook

Wednesday, January 17

"Remember some interview subjects may be hostile due to the nature of the story. It is your job as a reporter to make them understand you are not there to judge; but to tell a complete story you need to see both sides of the conflict."

—Mrs. G.

I looked up the word *disadvantage* online. Found this:

Disadvantaged—

Adjective

1. Lacking the normal or usual necessities and comforts of life such as proper housing, educational opportunities, job security, adequate medical care

Example: The government extends aid to disadvantaged minorities.

noun—

Disadvantaged persons collectively.

Example: The senator advocates increased funding for federal programs that aid the disadvantaged.

16

Miss Addy was dressed and waiting when I entered the kitchen.

"Why are you up so early?" It wasn't even five a.m. Grandpa was taking me to Wetzel's. Time to bake the cupcakes. I yawned. My schedule was definitely getting the best of me.

"I'm coming with you," she said. She gripped her purse strap to her body and the fabric of her puffy coat sleeves made a swish-swish sound.

Then I noticed she was carrying something. She turned and held it out to me.

"I thought you might like it. It's a cookbook that my grandmother handed down to me," she said.

"Miss Addy, I can't take your cookbook!" I held it

like a mystical tablet in a fairy tale. Its cover was red-and-white checked and inside, the pages were marked up with notations. At the back were several handwritten notes and recipes. One of them had the date 1947 written on top. She must have had this since, like, forever.

"Of course you can take it," she said. "It's mine. Now it's yours. Tradition."

"What about Mom?"

We shared a look. She said, "I love my daughter, but no way is she getting her non-cooking hands on my cherished family cookbook. Now go on before we're late. I want to see where you do all your cookin'!"

You know what? I was too tired to argue. We went outside, into the bitingly cold air, our cheeks instantly staining a bright red. Grandpa was already outside warming up the car. It took the car longer to heat up than it took us to drive to the bakeshop.

At the bakery, I introduced Miss Addy to Mrs. Wetzel. Grandpa grunted his usual hello. Mrs. W. was used to him by now. We all moved into the store space where I always brought Grandpa coffee and something to nibble. Miss Addy told Mrs. Wetzel she wanted to work with me, if it was all right with her. It was.

I could tell Miss Addy had something on her mind, but I was grateful that she just worked alongside me for an hour. Whenever I came into the bakery I went on autopilot. Bowls. Ingredients. Dry goods. Butter, eggs, cream cheese out of the fridge.

Recipes were clear instructions. Do this. Then this. Then that. And—voila! A cupcake is born. I couldn't help thinking that it was like writing computer code. An algorithm. Do one thing, then another, and another. A pattern. It made me feel proud to make that connection.

However, what didn't make me feel proud was remembering my last trip to Price. As much as I'd enjoyed the basketball game and meeting all the parents—even hanging out with Shania—being called an "Oreo" to my face made me feel that just because of where I lived I was less African American than they were. It did not feel great.

When I was removing my last batch of cupcakes for the morning from the oven, Miss Addy came over with the most heavenly looking ganache I'd ever seen.

"It's chocolate peanut butter," she said. "My own recipe. It's in the cookbook. Dip your chocolate cupcakes in it and they'll taste like Reese's Peanut Butter Cups."

183

"Looks great," I said.

We set about converting plain chocolate cupcakes into creamy works of art. She said, "I'm really sorry, little queen, that your plan backfired the way it did. I feel responsible. Like maybe I should've talked you out of it."

"No, Miss Addy!" I cried, spinning around. "It wasn't your fault. Mom's the one who went all postal."

Mom and I had been moping around since our blowup, and it was making me tired. Besides, I had other stuff on my mind.

Miss Addy smiled. "Well, my girl, you're sweet to say it, but both of you have such strong personalities."

"Daddy says we're too much alike," I said, standing back to get a good look at the row of freshly dipped cupcakes.

Miss Addy wiped her hands on a towel and stepped back, as well. "Funny, that's what her father used to say about us!"

We both laughed, and when my beautiful grandmother reached out to pull me into a hug, I leaned into it.

Before I could tell my mouth to do otherwise, I asked:

"Uh, Miss Addy, has anyone ever called you an Oreo?"

Her response was a bark of laughter. I frowned.

"Child, I've been called some of everything, including Oreo. It's sad when some black folks make others feel like being African American is a private club. And if you don't act a certain way or live a certain way, you aren't welcome."

She knew exactly how I felt. "So you know how it feels?" I said.

"Absolutely! Honey, just remember, no one can make you feel bad about yourself without your permission."

"What does that mean?"

"It means, until you stop beating up on yourself for having more than those children at that school you visited, they will continue to push you around by making you feel guilty," she said.

"But Miss Addy, I don't think that's it. I mean, they think because of where I live, how I live, how I talk and dress, that somehow that makes me different from them. Not black like them." I took a breath. My heart was hammering and I was beginning to feel a little nauseated. But I went on.

"And the truth is, back when I first met them or whatever, I sort of felt like I wasn't like them; and they weren't like me. So does that make me an Oreo? A black person who looks black on the outside but wants to be white on the inside? I mean, when Grandma Diane was alive, she always made me feel proud to be black. I felt like a little strong black woman, because that's what she called me. Now? Well, I'm not sure how to feel."

She moved closer, catching my face in her warm hands.

"My little queen, you should feel free to be the strong black woman you were meant to be. You are blessed. I struggled and made sacrifices so that my daughter could have opportunities that I didn't. Now she has a family and can provide a home for you that she didn't have. Did being strapped for cash and working hard make us more black?"

I frowned again, unable to answer. When she said it like that, she made me realize that the Price kids were trying to make a point—that if you're hardworking with few resources, that makes you a real black person. But if you're living in the suburbs working for your dreams, you're somehow less black.

That thinking was no better than me thinking that just because you lived in a disadvantaged neighborhood, it meant you were ghetto. Just so you know, I'm never using the *G* word again. (Good-bye, "Go Ask Darnell." You are not funny anymore!)

She kissed me on the cheek as the revelation dawned in my eyes. I squeezed her and said, "Thank you for everything!"

We got back to work, dipping the cupcakes in ganache, then topping them with rich, creamy chocolate frosting. I thought about Toya loaning me the *Raisin in the Sun* DVD.

"Miss Addy, have you ever heard of a movie called *A Raisin in the Sun*? I watched it recently."

Her eyes grew round and shiny.

"When I was ten years old, my mama and her Alpha Kappa Alpha sorority sisters took me with them to see the production on Broadway. It was such a huge honor and one of the most amazing experiences of my life."

We discussed the play. How it was about a black family in Chicago who received a large sum of money, enough to leave their rough neighborhood and buy a nice home in a white neighborhood. Only to find out the neighbors decided before meeting them, without seeing them, that they weren't wanted.

"It was the first play by an African American woman

to appear on Broadway," I said, remembering what I'd read online.

Grandma twirled a freshly dipped cupcake until the ganache dripped slowly into the bowl. She nodded, saying, "Back then, that was a big, big deal. After the play came out, we learned a lot about why she wrote it. The story in the movie was influenced by her life. Her family had been part of a class-action lawsuit claiming they were being denied housing based on race."

I remembered what Buffalo Bob said and his wife's essay. Ghettos came about because minorities were pushed into certain areas. Wherever minorities lived, regardless of how nice or grimy, it was called a ghetto.

In a soft voice fraught with the shame and guilt that had been weighing on me like a heavy meal, I told her about Price Academy. How scared I'd been to go.

"I was stereotyping other black people based on where they live," I said in a hoarse whisper. Eyes filling up, I went on. "I'd never thought of myself as that kind of person, but I guess I was. But being called 'Oreo' and treated like I was so different, well, it's made me really feel confused."

Miss Addy said, "Honey, I have a lot of black history in these old bones. I've seen a lot over the years. What I want you to get out of everything that has happened is we as black folks in America watch the same news and study the same history in school as everybody else. Don't beat yourself up about getting the same message."

"What message?" I asked.

"That we should be afraid of black folks or, at the very least, amused by them," she said softly.

"Miss Addy, I don't go around at school thinking about who's black and who isn't or anything like that. To be honest, sometimes, like when we're learning stuff in history about slavery, it makes me feel funny. Bad. I don't want to see myself like that. I don't want to think about my ancestors that way."

She grinned and shook her head.

"Baby, there's more to black history than slavery and poverty. Look at the story you're writing for the paper. A bunch of educated black women coming together for the betterment of other black women. I can't think of anything more positive and beautiful. Remember, just because you've learned part of the story of how our country came to be great, it doesn't mean you know the whole story. People of all colors have contributed to our fine nation in ways you can't yet understand.

"Find their stories. Share their culture. Make your life and the lives of your children stronger by knowing more," she said.

I hugged her, then told her I'd just gotten an idea for Black History Month. A story for the *Blueberry* and a Presidents' Day challenge for the sixth grade. I explained what I was thinking.

"I love it!" she exclaimed.

So did I!

I ☆ I ☆ I ☆ I

I spoke with Mr. and Mrs. G. about my ideas.

They gave me the green light, which made me let out a huge sigh of relief.

Plan number one involved my friend Click and our latest mini-movie with the LEGOs. Once a week we put together funny little stories—stop-motion movies that wind up being about a minute long. However, they can take hours, days to finish.

Since we didn't need it until the Friday before Presidents' Day in February, we still had time. But with my schedule so packed, I thought it would be best to start early.

We used to record our mini-movies at Click's house until Mrs. G. found space for us in a room that used to be a radio station at the school.

It had windows that looked out into the hallway. Now, whenever we worked on our movie sets, kids could walk by and watch us. I always liked that. Click, well, he was so focused, I don't know if he much noticed the noses pressed against the glass.

"What's up with this idea?" he asked. So I explained my idea for a Presidents' Day tribute with a mini-movie.

Instead of doing a funny little LEGO story about what it's like to be in middle school, I wanted us to do a story about the Fair Housing Act.

"Say whaaaaaaat?" asked Click. He did this exaggerated pull to one side with his long body that made me bark out a laugh. I gave him a playful push.

"Okay, hear me out." I told him about my embarrassing education at the newspaper office concerning the origins of the word *ghetto*.

He said, "I never knew that the word *ghetto* started

way back in the fifteen hundreds. Being Mexican American, I thought the same thing. The only time I see anything about ghettos, it's either brown people like me or black people like you. But Jewish people, too?"

"The word *ghetto* did not start with our people," I said.

"But how are we going to do a LEGO movie about a housing act and make it work?"

"It's called the Fair Housing Act of 1968. It made it illegal for anyone to discriminate against a person because of their race, religion, or whatever when it comes to buying or renting a house," I explained.

My idea was this:

We'd set up a neighborhood and make these little FOR SALE signs to place on the lawns. The mini-figures would go from house to house and get the door shut in their faces.

With his eyes widened, Click jumped in:

"And in between frames, we can insert shots—photos of sixth graders—holding signs about discrimination."

"That's right! And we can add something about how calling people or places ghetto isn't cool, especially when you only know half the story!" I said.

You might not know this about Click, but he loves his

LEGOs and he loves his stop-motion movies. And when he gets a really awesome story idea he can do with the mini-figures and buildings, that boy gets hyped!

"B, are you serious right now?" he practically shouted, jumping up and down. People outside the window were laughing. "This is going to be crazy good, girl!" After that, we gathered the pieces we kept locked in the storage closet.

We agreed that while Click set up the neighborhood, I would get started on the text that would go with the movie. Then we got to work.

An hour later we had taken about two hundred pictures, but we still had many more to go.

"Wanna see how it looks so far?" Click asked.

"Absolutely," I said.

He used his phone to take the pictures, then plugged that directly into the laptop. The video-editing program organized the photos and when you played them all together, it made the pieces appear to move.

He hit a few keys on his laptop and the little movie started to replay. No matter how many times we did it, the movies always blew my mind a little. They were amazing to see all put together like that.

A knock at the glass practically scared the snot out of me. Click and I both turned sharply and saw three faces pressed to the hallway window. Two kids from our journalism class and some other kid. They all must've been on the basketball team and were coming from practice.

"Yo, man! That's dope!" came the muffled voice of the tallest one. "Can we come in?"

Click looked at me. I shrugged. The area where we were working wasn't that big, but we could probably squeeze them in. I nodded and Click went to ask permission from Mrs. G., who always stayed late when we worked after school.

A few seconds later he came back with the three sweaty basketball players from the window. Did you ever notice that no matter what they're doing, boys are just plain loud? Middle school boys especially.

They had just come from practice, so they didn't smell so good, either!

"Hey, President Girl!" said one of the boys.

"Hey," I said, glancing up.

"So what's the story this week?" asked another one of the boys.

When I looked up, the one who'd called me President Girl was just staring at me. I narrowed my eyes at him and asked, "Can I do something for you?"

Then he did a long, slow grin. "Well, yeah. You could—"

I cut him off. One look at his face and I could see he was having some puberty problems.

"Boy, please!" I said with an eye roll.

The other boys, Click included, started laughing and saying, "Ahh-ha, man. She shut you down!"

I laughed, too, and after that everything got chill. Sure, everyone wanted to work near the window, so we were pressed into a tight space that was beginning to smell like gym socks and corn chips. However, the boys were really into it. They even helped us with the set and moving the pieces.

Which left me free to concentrate on what to write between film clips. As much as I was into my project, I started to feel this tightness in my chest. That usually happened when I had a lot going on.

And I always had a lot going on.

Presidents' Day was right around the corner. Not only did that mean completing this movie project, it also meant finishing another project for the *Blueberry* that I'd suggested to Mrs. G.

Not to mention, Neptune was coming to Detroit that weekend.

Oh, and did I mention our cheer team's first exhibition was the Saturday before Presidents' Day?

Ugh!

Then there was my SheCodes program interview. McSweater Vest told us he'd set up interviews over the phone with the woman who co-founded the SheCodes foundation.

So much to do! Add cooking at the bakery a few times a week, homework, and cheerleading practice and woooo-goodness! It was getting rough.

That thought made me think about the biggest issue in my life—Mom.

The more I looked at my to-do list the more I had begun to realize that she was—*gulp!*—right. Going to a parent and admitting you're wrong and they're right is like asking for medicine. It's just wrong!

Still, I was determined to figure something out. I didn't like walking around the house being extra polite and not acting like us.

Then I felt something on my neck and realized it was someone's breath. I spun and found one the guys staring down at my hair bun.

"What are you doing?" I asked, giving him a shove.

"Girl, you strong!" declared one of the other boys. Ugh! It's like being in a room full of puppies.

I was no longer paying them any attention. I was looking at my caller ID screen.

"Hello," I said. My heart had begun pounding. My throat felt dry.

"Brianna, hey, this is Mom," came the voice.

"Baby, I'm picking you up from school today instead of Granddad," she said. Then came the four most dreaded words a mother can say to her kid:

"We need to talk!"

Reporter's Notebook

Wednesday, January 24

Does a girl have to be a genius to be good at computer science?

"To be a good computer scientist, a young lady only needs to be curious, like solving problems, and want to help or change the world. That's really it! The way that computer science programs in college are set up, she should also learn to like math (because she'll take a good amount of it in college)."

—Dr. Jakita Thomas, PhD, Philpott-WestPoint Stevens Associate Professor of Computer Science and Software Engineering at Auburn University and 2016 recipient of the Presidential Early Career Award for Scientists and Engineers

Technology note:

What kind of jobs can you get with a computer science degree?

- Database administrator
- Games developer
- IT consultant
- Web designer
- Web developer
- Digital copywriter

Hmm...

I've never heard of most of these jobs before. Entry-level, which means when you first start out, pay is around $52,000 a year; but the average salary for someone with a computer science career is about $80,000 a year. Not a million dollars, but not bad.

17

My heart beat so hard I thought it would knock out the car window.

Thankfully, the car ride was short. The window was safe. My heartbeat, however, did not slow down.

She stopped at my favorite restaurant, the Chili's on 10 Mile Road. Uh-oh. An unexpected Mommy-and-me date at my favorite restaurant. That had trouble written all over it.

We'd placed our orders and exchanged minor chit-chat. It took about everything I had not to jump over the table and say sorry, sorry, sorry, please don't send me to military school!

However, Mom spoke first. She surprised me, reaching across the table and taking both my hands into hers.

"So, baby girl, let's get down to it," Mom said.

She drew a deep breath, then said, "I'm so sorry about our blowup. I know you get excited and just want to do and try some of everything, and I love that about you."

A HUGE lump formed in my throat. She was apologizing to me?

"No, Mom..." I tried cutting in. She squeezed my fingers a little harder, shaking her head.

"Please, I know you want to speak, but let me finish." She drew a big breath and let it out. She told me it was her job to worry about me, protect me, and provide for me. She said she loved how motivated I was by life, but, as I was learning, sometimes I got too involved and wanted to do too much at the same time.

"Mom, I'm sorry, too. I have so many things going on right now, I guess I can't imagine adding an online business. But you're right, I want to do everything so much."

Mom laughed. "Girl, I know you. And you, Brianna Justice, gotta learn how to chill once in a while. Pace yourself."

We both took sips from our drinks and dipped our salty chips into the salsa. After a few minutes, Mom's expression went soft and she gave me a funny look.

Uh-oh. There was more.

"Brianna, my boss had a long talk with me yesterday. If I'm going to accept the job in D.C., they need my decision this week. Like, tomorrow. I've talked to your dad and Katy. Now I'm talking to you."

My body snapped into rigid attention. Nerve endings zinged and fired. No, no, no, no! Not right now when everything was getting good again.

She reached out and grabbed my hands again.

"You girls, your dad, you've been my whole life. But in families, sacrifices sometimes have to be made. It's scary. It might not seem fair, but it happens. The way you feel about your journalism, cheering, baking, and wanting to start a business, that's how I feel about what I do.

"Getting this promotion is a huge deal for me. For all of us. Please say you'll think about it. That you'll try to..."

I was shaking my head. "Mom, please don't make me leave. Please?"

She came around and slid in beside me, gathering me close to her like she did when I was little. She rocked me back and forth. I know. Terribly embarrassing for a class president and future Pulitzer Prize–winning journalist. But I didn't care.

"Oh, baby, try not to take it so hard. Do you think it would really be that bad if you had to leave after sixth grade?"

"YES!" I cried. "Mom, please. Just ask your boss for a little more time. Think about it. I'll do anything. ANYTHING! Mom, I'm not ready. I'm just not ready."

Finally, she let out a long sigh. Pulling away from me, she looked into my eyes and said, "All right, Brianna. I'll tell him I need more time. But I need you to really give this some thought."

I dried my face with a napkin. "What if after I take some time I decide I really don't want to go. Would we really stay?"

"Baby, I honestly don't know. I don't want you to be miserable. I think we can all be happy in D.C. if you give it a chance," she said.

So there was a chance! My heart felt all warm and glowy. I said, "I'll think about all the reasons it might not be so bad to leave, if you'll think about all the reasons it would be awesome to stay. Deal?"

"Deal," she said. She tried to smile, but her eyes had that worried Mom look. Was I being selfish?

I couldn't think about it. I just wasn't ready to say good-bye to my friends and my life. Not yet!

I☆I☆I☆I

We had a few more days to get ready for the SheCodes workshop.

The story had to be good. Better than good. Spectacular!

Only, now I wasn't worried about being better than Julian Berger or anything like that. I was really curious about how the conference would go, who would be there, and what I might learn.

See, the more I researched careers in technology, the more excited I became. Weird, right? I'd learned a lot about computers and coding. Thinking about the Mom situation, I wished I could come up with a computer program to tell me what to do or how to act.

McSweater Vest picked us up like always and took us to the *Freep*. I'd gotten really nervous because today we had appointments to talk to the women who created the program. In the car, I started asking practice questions:

1. Is there a certain way you should talk to professional experts?
2. How do I know what questions to ask?
3. What if the women I was supposed to interview thought I was just some kid who didn't know what she was doing?

"Whoa!" McSweater Vest said with a hearty laugh. I had to laugh, too. Maybe I was getting a little too hyped. I'd learned that the computer science field—and the science field as a whole—is full of African American women. The kind of bright, dignified, on-top-of-their-game women who did not resemble the portrayals of black women in memes or joke videos.

The kind of black woman I definitely wanted to be, whether I studied computer science or not!

He said, "I'm so happy to see you getting into your subject matter. It always helps when a journalist is really passionate about the story they have to tell."

Red high-fived me.

We parked and did our usual greetings with J., the security dude in the green blazer. Not long after we arrived, Buffalo Bob came rumbling over, driving his swivel chair again.

"How's it going, Lois Lanes?" he asked, the usual big grin plastered across his face.

Turns out, if you're a girl reporter, folks will call you Lois Lane. A lot. Well, there were worse things than a Superman reference, I supposed.

I smiled at him. We both said we were doing fine, but then I had a sudden need to tell him something.

"Um, thank you," I said timidly. I was grateful that he'd cared enough about me, my story, and my attitude that he'd gotten in my face. It shook me up that day, but I was glad it had happened.

His bushy reddish brown eyebrows knit into a caterpillar-ish clump. "Thanks for what?" he said. Before I could answer, he shook his hands in a *go away* gesture. "Reporters help reporters. Professional courtesy!"

I grinned.

Then in another fit of conscience, I turned to my mentor and blurted:

"Ever since you started mentoring me, I've referred to you as McSweater Vest in my head. That was rude. Sorry...uh, Mr., *um*, McShea."

Red giggled. "You are funny when you're contrite."

I slid her a glance and asked, "Language arts vocabulary word?"

"You know it!" she said.

Now we were all laughing, including Mr. McShea. He said, "Oh, I'm well aware of your nickname for me. You slipped and called me that several times. No worries. I like my sweater vests. Besides, with your white shirts, hair buns, and cardigans, I figured we make a fine pair!"

I looked down. I was wearing skinny dark-wash jeans with a white shirt and a fitted black-and-red cardigan. I looked down at my outfit and then up at his.

Well, for goodness' sake! We really were dressed alike. Now we all burst out laughing again until one of the editors across the room scowled at us and Mr. McShea said we should get to work.

"Girls, we are officially on deadline," he said. We were writing two stories—the first was running Saturday morning, the day of the program. It would be the bigger story.

Then we were attending the conference and writing a

follow-up. Both of those pieces were running in the *Freep*'s online edition, along with a commentary piece by me.

Buffalo Bob hung around, too, lending his insight.

Today he wore a T-shirt that read:

"IF THERE IS A BOOK THAT YOU WANT TO READ, BUT IT HASN'T BEEN WRITTEN YET, YOU MUST BE THE ONE TO WRITE IT."

—*TONI MORRISON*

Toni Morrison is a famous African American female author. Buffalo Bob had a lot of those kinds of shirts.

"Hey, Mr. Buffalo, why do you wear so many shirts with sayings by black people?"

He drew his neck back and peered at me.

With a bark of laughter, he said, "Because black women are the mothers of modern civilization." He said it like, *Duh?*

He went on:

"Scientists are always discovering ancient bones or human remains. The oldest ones come from Africa. There are remains and artifacts showing a very modern structured civilization dating back two hundred thousand years in Africa. Black women were strong and powerful long before Europe or Europeans even existed."

He grinned.

I grinned.

No matter what the girls at Price said, I was part of that ancestry. They didn't get to describe the kind of person I was or the person I wanted to be! I wasn't going to let them make me feel bad about myself or my favorite cookies. I loved my Oreos—with white milk, too!!

"Maybe someone should make you an honorary black woman," I said.

Then up walked a tall woman, a columnist whose face I recognized from her picture in the paper. She had killer cheekbones and a tidy little Afro, like Toya's. She walked up behind him and placed a hand on his shoulder.

"Sugar, I dubbed Buffalo Bob an honorary black woman a long time ago. He is down for the struggle and up for the empowerment," she said.

Buffalo Bob grinned, raised a fist, and said, "Right on!" Then he pointed to the saying on his shirt again.

"That doesn't just go for writing books. It goes for all kinds of storytelling," he said. Poking me in the shoulder with his finger, he said, "You *be* the change! We don't know where potential news will turn up, but when you see something happening that needs a light shined on it, shine on, little mama, shine on!"

Then in true Buffalo Bob fashion, he did a hand explosion like—*poof!*—and then drove his swivel chair away, away, away!

Reporter's Notebook

How to interview hostile subjects:

Not everyone who makes news wants to speak to the media. Still, as reporters, you have an obligation to get the best evidence from the most knowledgeable source. When someone is combative, angry, or confrontational, a good reporter will defuse the situation.

Try letting the subject know that you understand their feelings. Do not push or try to match their agitation. Be in control of your interview, not controlled by the emotions of the subject.

1. Be friendly, polite, and courteous.
2. If someone gets harsh or aggressive, remind them that you understand how tough their situation is but you're just there to do a job.
3. Tell them you need their help. When you make people part of the solution, it can sometimes redirect them away from the problem.

18

We were on the mats. Feet bare. Stretching. A competitive cheerleader's life is all about flexibility. Red and I were side by side, pressing to the floor in splits.

"I can't believe it's almost time to turn in our stories," I said. It was one thing to be on deadline for Mrs. G. It was quite another to feel the pressure of writing a real news story for a real newspaper.

"Me neither," Red said. "But I'm really proud of all the hard work we've done. And I'm proud of you, Justice. I know you had some bumps in the road with this story."

We smiled at each other. I looked away, drew a long sigh, then faced her again.

"I can't believe how crazy I've been," I said. "Venus was right, you know? I am dumb!"

"Not just you. Look at all the kids at school who watch those videos and think it's hilarious," Red said.

"But you never did."

She shrugged. "I told you, my parents were always very open about stereotypes and discrimination."

"So are mine!" I said. We sat facing each other. I pressed the soles of my feet together, knees bouncing gently up and down; so did she. I went on:

"What gets me, though, is that as an African American kid, my parents taught me about tolerating people who looked different and expecting that respect in return. But no one really tells you to beware of stereotyping people who look like you."

Red gave a sly, lopsided grin. She said, "Did y'all know my mama was considered white trailer trash?"

"RED!" I shouted. Coach T. boomeranged me with one of her sharply arched brows. I lowered my voice. "Red, how can you say a thing like that? You can't say that about someone—especially your own mama."

She let out a whoop of laughter. "Justice, you should

see the look on your face. Look, the way you feel right now, all uncomfortable and sorta icky. Well, that's how I feel when you and other kids go around yukking it up about folks being *ghetto*."

I gulped. I'd never thought about it like that. Then I burst out laughing. *Ghetto* doesn't even sound right coming out of her mouth. So weird.

Red said, "My mama did grow up in a trailer park. In a dusty, poor area of Texas where she was called white trash on a regular basis. It wasn't black kids or Hispanics or anybody else doing the name calling, either. It was other white kids. But she managed to earn a scholarship to a prestigious private school, then she became a dancer and later Miss Texas and second runner-up to Miss America. And then she went to college, married my dad, and ran her own dance school. She did amazing things, especially from where she started."

I nodded. I thought about Mom's father dying when she was young, her having to work her way through college before landing her dream job, becoming a wife, a mother. Kids don't think about that kind of thing a lot, but sometimes amazingness can be found close to home.

A little itch of doubt wormed into my thoughts. Mom getting that promotion was a big deal. But I wasn't ready to go. Not yet. Maybe not ever!

We were just about finished with our warmup when Lori, Sandra, and a few other girls joined us. It was pretty chill. Most of us were feeling the pressure. Our exhibition was only a few weeks away and we were getting jumpy, no pun intended.

Then Tracy joined us, tossed her perfectly even dark twists, and placed a hand on her hip. She said, "So, Brianna, you're not going back to the ghetto, right? That place is so—"

But I was on my feet and in her face before she could finish that foolishness.

"Tracy, you and I are African American like a lot of folks on the east side," I said with such emphasis, she took a step back. But I wasn't finished.

"I'll admit, I got caught up in calling people names and thinking it was funny, but those kids over there, they deserve our respect!"

"You don't know what you're talking about!" Tracy shot back. "I don't care what you say!"

"And you don't know what you're talking about. You

215

don't even know where the word *ghetto* comes from. It means—"

"I don't need you telling me any definitions. I don't care what you say, I'm nothing like them!"

WHEEERT!

The whistle. Coach T. appeared beside us, whistle between her teeth, blowing hard.

"Girls! What is the problem?" Several voices spoke at once as we all tried to explain.

After several stops and starts, Coach T. was getting the picture. She took a moment, then looked around at us, her gaze going from face to face. Finally, she asked, "How many of you have an opinion about people living over on the east side?"

Several hands went up.

She nodded, then led us toward a huge red mat beside the big wall mirror. Once we were all plopped down on the floor mat—me with steam still coming out of my ears—Coach T. smiled her bright, cheerleader smile.

"Girls, I'm so proud of you. It's time we had this discussion." Of all the things I'd been expecting, that wasn't one of them.

Tracy grumbled, "All I'm saying is just because

Brianna went over and met a few kids who seemed nice, that doesn't mean the east side is a good place. Ghetto is ghetto." She huffed and sat with her back to the mirror, arms folded, face turned away from mine.

"Guess that makes me ghetto," Coach T. said.

Say what?

"I grew up right next to where Price Academy is. Only, back then, we didn't have a charter school. We had a collection of failing schools that made it really hard to get the same kind of education as other kids," she said.

"But I thought you said you went to college?" Tracy asked suspiciously.

Lori and Sandra looked as if they might pass out.

Coach T. said, "I did go to college. Georgia Tech. I have a dual degree in computer science and graphic design."

My eyes grew wide. She was a techie?

She pulled into a deep side lean. "Hey, now! You all don't have to act like just because I'm a cheerleading beast, I can't get my tech on, too!"

That made us all laugh and it sort of broke the tension. For the next thirty minutes, instead of drills,

217

burpees, routines, and stamina exercises, Coach T. talked to us about her life.

She told us her mother worked as an aide in a nursing home. Her father died when she was still an infant. Her mother remarried and had two other children. Then her stepfather walked out.

"Believe me," she said, "we did not have a lot when I was growing up. Sometimes if my siblings and I didn't eat at school, we didn't eat. Period."

She paused, letting that sink in. I could feel the way we all sort of gasped when she said it. It was hard to imagine ever not being able to get enough to eat at home. Mom and Dad always kept our cupboards stuffed.

Coach T. said, "It killed me, though, to see how not being able to take better care of us affected my mom. She started working two jobs. I swear to goodness, between fourth grade and my high school graduation I barely saw her. My half-sister babysat us a lot so Mama could work."

"Did your sister go to college?" Lori asked.

She shook her head. "She couldn't afford to. She was too busy taking care of us." Coach T. sighed. "But my brother and I went to college. He just graduated from Central Michigan with an engineering degree. I got my degree in computer science and graphic design. I'm actually helping out with a workshop at an event for inner-city girls on Saturday."

Well, I could've fainted.

Red and I exchanged glances. "You mean the SheCodes workshop?" I asked.

"Yes, you've heard of it?"

Red and I looked at each other with huge wide-eyed expressions. In a tumble and jumble of words, together we launched into an explanation of how we were working on a story about the program and we'd interviewed all sorts of people.

"That's how this whole thing about Price Academy and the east side started," Red said, almost out of breath from talking so fast. "Justice and I were going there and then a few girls here started acting like we were headed to a war zone, and then..."

Coach T. nodded. Then she looked from Red to me and said, "You do realize that part of the reason the girls have those perceptions about low-income neighborhoods is due to the media."

Well, that sat me back on my heels. *Say what?*

"When I was growing up over there, a huge fight broke

out at the high school. The police came, and parents tried to get involved. Before you knew it, the police were lobbing tear gas into the crowds and using those protective shields. On the news that night, a reporter actually called my neighborhood a war zone. My home," she said.

She told us that no matter how many people in her neighborhood volunteered, helped paint over graffiti, clean up parks, older women organizing to help working mothers who couldn't afford day care for little ones— none of that was mentioned in the media. All anyone talked about for months was how it had gotten so bad on the east side that it was "a war zone."

I felt chilled thinking about it.

After a moment, I ventured, "But Coach, you can't fault the media for reporting what happened. That was what happened, right?"

"Sure, but I can fault the media for how it was reported. Girls, look, one of the things I hope Coach Kristy and I can teach you if we don't teach anything else is to work hard, show up, be present, and take control. But we also want you to ask questions, learn from each other, and learn from everyone around you. Respect your competitors and respect yourselves." She sighed. Then continued:

"As young women, you all will face stereotyping based on your gender, your looks, your weight, how you carry yourselves. People will line up to tell you what you can and cannot do."

She turned to me and Red and said, "And as journalists, you'll face biases on what to cover and how. All I'm saying is, part of everyone's responsibilities to their communities is to reject the narrative until you gather your own facts. Somebody starts talking smack about someone or something you aren't educated on, reject it until you get your own proof."

After the pep talk, Sandra and Lori apologized, saying they hadn't meant to hurt anyone's feelings. They admitted that the opinions they held were based on what they'd heard and been told, not what they'd learned for themselves.

Tracy, on the other hand, flounced off, still mad about whatever. Guess she needed to figure some things out for herself first. What could I say? I'd been there.

I☆I☆I☆I

Two hours later, Red leaned into her splits, touching her chest to her front thigh. Ballerinas were tough. I felt like my body was melting from the inside out. Still, in

221

my efforts to please Coach T. with a perfect scorpion pose for the exhibition, I strained my muscles, reached behind me, and grabbed my toes, tugging my foot closer and closer to the back of my head. Ow! Feel the burn!

Red asked, "Are you nervous? About writing the story? About the event on Saturday?"

After a few seconds of holding my foot, the back of my thigh shook. The muscle felt like it was on fire. I breathed in, and out.

"What I am nervous about," I whispered, not wanting anyone else in the WORLD to hear what I was saying, "is that Neptune wants to come to our exhibition."

Red, who was now out of her splits and sitting on her butt with her heels pressed together and her legs flat to the floor, glanced up.

With a wide grin on her face she declared, "Well, Justice, that's wonderful. Oooo! I think someone is starting to really like-like someone else."

"Shh!" I said.

She smiled, saying, "Seriously, I think you should be happy he wants to hang out. And that you guys are friends." The smile struggled to stay on her face as she continued, "Since you'll be moving up there in the summer, it'll be nice having a friend nearby."

I'd released my foot and was now sitting in front of her like a mirror image. We sat like that, facing each other, not speaking. Finally, I said, "We're not moving! Well, not definitely!"

She gave me a look.

"What?" I sputtered. "I don't want to think about leaving. I can't. I won't."

"So," she said, "instead, let's concentrate on how much friendship we can squeeze into the next few months. Whatever the future brings, let's just focus on being there for each other and being AWESOME together!"

She leaned forward and so did I. We had the most ridiculous hug—rocking back and forth while sitting crisscross applesauce. Red was my friend. Even though we met only a few months ago, we've gotten really close.

How could I even think about leaving?

Reporter's Notebook

Friday, January 26

Writing news features with multiple subjects:

"The first thing that I try to do is visualize the story, thinking of it as a play with multiple acts. Then I try to visualize my characters, how each of them fits into the larger puzzle or storyline. I approach easy subjects first. I find that they help me prepare for my larger or more complex subjects. By the time I get to my main "characters" I have a good sense of the story and what are the right questions to ask. Then I quickly sit down to write the one scene or moment that stayed with me the most."

—Audra Burch, enterprise correspondent,
national staff, *New York Times*

19

The jitteriness started in my heart.

And it spread all the way to my toes.

Red and I were pressed close to each other in the *Free Press* newsroom. All our notes were spread across the desktop. We separated everything into categories:

1. Price Academy girls
2. Two interviews with girls from other schools
3. Miss Talia Newsome, the teacher representative for SheCodes
4. Teachers, such as Mr. Hardaway at Price and our new science teacher, Miss Miata, who had some interesting things to say
5. The women scientists who organized the events

On top of the interviews, we had a lot of data—numbers and figures, percentages and real numbers, values and statistics. It was a lot to digest.

"The numbers are important," Mr. McShea reminded us, "but remember, the real star of this piece is the impact, the meaning this workshop could have for the community."

We nodded. Organizing our school interviews and going over them again, we decided to review our interviews with the girls and look for the quotes and statements that stood out the most.

"I really thought this was a good one," I said, indicating with my finger one of my favorite interviews that day. The quote I thought was best:

"I first got involved because Miss Newsome told my grandma about it and she made me start coming to the science club after school. But then I started to like coming. Miss newsome helped me get better at math and that gave me more confidence. I want to be an actress, but she told me that earning a science or technology degree didn't mean I had to give up on acting. A lot of celebrities have degrees. Some go on to use them, others don't. Most of all, I want to do something that makes me feel good about myself and helps my family. Living on the east side, sometimes all you think you can do is get in trouble. I'm glad Miss newsome has shown me there are other things, too. I'm excited to see what I learn from the workshop."

—Christyanna Webb, seventh grader, Price Academy

Red then shared her favorite quote. "She reminded me a lot of you, Justice!"

"My name is Nadia Marie Robinson, and the reason I want to attend the workshop and learn about computers is because I want to design computer games. I want to make better games than the ones my brother plays—the kind where you only break the law and shoot at the police. We got enough of that going on for real. My games are gonna be better than that and I'm going to make a LOT of money!"

—Nadia Marie Robinson, sixth grader, Price Academy

"Okay, she does sound like me a little," I admitted. We laughed. Of course, both of us heard Mrs. G.'s voice in the back of our minds about the importance of including "visuals" so we made sure we had photos of the girls.

Then we got down to the good stuff, going over our interviews with the event organizers.

I had spoken with Dr. Quincy Brown. She was in charge of, like, all the programs for STEM—science, technology, engineering, and math. Even though I participated in elementary, I've been too involved with other things since I got to middle school.

Anyway, it was so cool the way Dr. Brown, who is a lady, thank you very much, talked to me like a grown-up when she explained why programs that help disadvantaged kids also benefit society.

"I think of computer science as being important for everyone. The challenge has been that not enough of us—people of color—have been engaged in that space. More of us need to be here. What we bring, our culture, our wisdom and collective insights. We need to be involved with creating solutions to problems that affect us. What we bring to

the table needs to be shared with
everyone."

We'd talked about a movie that came out about these African American women scientists who helped with the NASA program and the nation's first moonwalk. I told her I'd been surprised to hear about it—even Mom and Dad had been surprised.

If black women played such a critical role in the success of America's space program, why was it so unknown until now?

"We've just let other people tell
our history. That's why so few people understand our contributions to
math, science, and computer technology."

Then I read another quote aloud, nodding to Buffalo Bob, who I could tell was dying to come over. With a broad grin on his face, he said, "I'm proud of you girls. This is good stuff. Can't wait to read it in the paper tomorrow."

Then Red and I dove into the story, clicking and typing and fretting and sweating. It was tougher than cheer practice, with an extra dose of fear thrown in. Deadlines for real newspapers are no joke.

But by six o'clock we'd been edited, questioned, grilled, double-checked, and practically interrogated for hidden statistics, misused quotes, and poor grammar.

Still, victory was ours. We won. The story went to press.

I☆I☆I☆I

Later that night we celebrated at my house with pizza. Red's mom and dad joined my crazy family, including Angel cat plus the variety of critters Katy kept stashed in various places around the house.

We ordered huge steaming pepperoni pizza pies, meat lovers, veggie, even that pineapple and ham garbage Dad loved. When we had everything spread out on the counters, we helped ourselves and camped out in the den.

"To our beautiful daughters," saluted Mr. Chastain, holding his meat lovers slice high in a toast. "We are so proud of both of you girls!"

"Cheers!" we all said.

Mom said, "So tomorrow's the big day, right? We finally get to see the fruits of all your labor?"

"I hope you guys like it. We worked really hard," I said, feeling uncharacteristically shy about it. Red and I had put so much time into the project, the idea of anyone thinking it was boring or unprofessional almost made me sick.

Almost.

Not so much, though, that it got in the way of my yummy pepperoni slice.

"You girls may not understand yet, but telling positive stories in the newspaper, especially about areas that see more than their fair share of negative press, is so important," Miss Addy said. I was glad she'd stayed after my disastrous plan blew up.

We all talked about everything and nothing, funny stuff, movies. When we turned on the television, a news update popped up. It was Yavonka Steele with Julian Berger.

"Turn it up! Turn it up!" I yelled.

Dad hit the volume button.

"Tonight at ten, investigative reporter Yavonka Steele goes undercover to expose a car theft ring. And this time, she's sharing the spotlight with her very own middle school mentee. Tune in tonight!"

Red and I exchanged glances.

Then I realized my whole family and the Chastains were staring at me.

I burst out laughing.

"Poor Julian," I said, meaning it. "He looked terrified." Then I got this tickle inside. I'd realized something. Yavonka Steele's news was flashy and in your face. But when I thought about spending time at Price Academy, meeting so many people, then writing stories that might in some small way improve how the kids feel about themselves and how the rest of Detroit feels about them, too, I knew feature writing was better for me than breaking news.

I glanced across the room at Mom. Did helping people as an FBI agent feel as important to her as my story made me feel? Would moving to D.C. help more people in need?

Mr. Chastain said, "Has this experience of working with journalists made a difference in terms of what you hope to do when you grow up?"

Red's cheeks were stuffed with pizza, so I went first.

"Um, I don't know. I mean, I was so excited about the idea of being a journalist. I thought I wanted to be a television newsperson. But now I think, maybe I wanted to be famous and rich more than I wanted to be a journalist," I said.

Miss Addy laughed. "Baby, there's nothing wrong with being famous or rich."

We all chuckled at that. I said, "I know. But after doing all this research about women in science and technology, I'm not saying that now I want to study computer science, but it's made me realize I can if I want to."

"Of course you can!" Mom said.

Miss Addy smiled, her eyes turning mischievous. She said, "Brianna, Red, I think you girls should come up to Mackinac Island for the summer. Spend some time working at my inn and in my fudge factory. Get a sense of truly owning your own business."

I glanced from Mom to Red. Mom said, "I think that would be excellent. Owning a business is a lot harder than one might think."

Okay, I got the message. Fortunately, Red had swallowed the massive lump of pizza she'd been chewing. She shifted the conversation back to reporting, saying,

"I really liked the journalism stuff more than I thought I would. I've already talked to Mrs. G. about starting my own blog and maybe hosting it through the school."

We bumped knuckles. She'd told me her plan last week and I thought it was awesome. I said, "And I've decided that tomorrow at the SheCodes workshop, I'm going to keep an open mind. If being a millionaire baker or a world-renowned journalist aren't in my future, who knows? Maybe being a famous scientist is."

Reporter's Notebook

"To be persuasive we must be believable; to be believable we must be credible; to be credible we must be truthful."

—Edward R. Murrow

"I've always wanted girls to just feel empowered. Just the sense of knowing they can create anything they want. Even if they don't know how exactly but knowing they can figure out exactly what they want; the fact that you know you can do it."

—Dr. Quincy Brown, Program Director, STEM Education Research, American Association for the Advancement of Science (AAAS)

20

It was finally the day of the SheCodes event.

I'd never seen anything like it. Even my leadership conference in D.C. paled by comparison.

Beautiful colorful banners hung from the ceilings. Nicely dressed women in their business best roamed around the wide-open space.

"Welcome!" called a black woman in a bright red dress. Her long hair was in tiny braids. As I looked around, I saw women everywhere. Women and girls. Black, Hispanic, Asian, and white. All colors, shades, and sizes. I even saw one of the ladies I'd interviewed at the basketball game. She had a little girl and three boys with her! No one said anything about the boys, so I guessed it was all good.

A long table sat outside a set of double doors. The women at the table asked our names and gave us name tags when Mr. McShea introduced us.

The woman looked at my name tag, then Red's. She said, "You're our young reporters. The write-up in the paper and online this morning was wonderful. You girls really did a great job!"

We beamed.

I had woken up before sunrise and raced down to the kitchen. Grandpa had already snagged the delivered copy of the paper. I had raced to the laptop set up in the kitchen. Both versions looked *so* professional. For a moment, I was certain Red and I would start getting bombarded with calls to do more professional stories.

It took a few seconds, but I managed to calm myself down.

Standing before these smart, innovative women, I stood straighter and did my best to absorb the feeling of empowerment permeating the air.

My hair had been brushed, gelled, and tugged into the best executive and professional bun I could manage. I wore a white shirt that was extra crisp. And today's cardigan was red. Finally, to set it off just a little bit more—*POW*—striped suspenders. Hey, I can have a playful side, too.

"Thank you, ma'am," we said.

She grinned. "We are going to do an opening ceremony inside. Then we'll break into four different rooms. Now, you are welcome to go to all four break-out sessions on specific areas of technology, or you can read through here"—she pushed a brochure my way—"and choose one. All of the sessions will be recorded, so if you'd like a copy of the recording, we can provide that. Also, in your packet, you'll have all the names of all the professionals dedicating their time to this worthy cause." She pushed a folder toward us filled with handouts, tips, and other conference essentials.

Then another arm encircled our shoulders and we looked up into the smiling face of Coach T.

"Hey, girls. Don't you look good in your big-girl clothes!" she almost cheered. We laughed and hugged her and she said we just had to pop into her web design course. We agreed, thanked the registration woman, and took our packets of information.

239

At nine a.m., a woman took center stage and began.

"My name is Gwendolyn deJongh," she said. "I am a lawyer, but I also hold a patent for an invention."

Ms. deJongh went on to explain her lifelong curiosity with gadgets. How in college she'd wanted to study law but never lost her desire to build things and take stuff apart to see how it worked.

"In college, I invented a device that would make my curls tighter," she said, indicating the spiraled-looking wand in her hand. "Now they are sold all over the world!"

Applause.

Several other women greeted us from the stage and shared stories of how they came to be in their fields. At twenty after, we were told we could participate in whichever hands-on learning program we wanted.

Red and I both turned to Mr. McShea. "Can we go to the one on robotics?" I asked.

"Sure. Do you think you'll want to stay with that one or move around?" We told him we wanted to go to the computer science workshops and learn about design in the afternoon.

For the next three hours, we not only learned how one young African American woman used a robot to help her design cars for General Motors, but we also got to use computers, modeling clay, tiny mechanical circuits, and soldering tools.

By the time it was over, we all had tiny little robotic arms that could perform basic functions. Next, we went to the computer science section. Our instructor told us: "To be in computer science you need to learn about the science of computing—algorithms, theories, and how data is stored and manipulated."

She told us that big words like *algorithm* didn't need to be scary. "It just means the order in which tasks are achieved. You come home from school. You drop your backpack on the floor. You open your fridge. You take out a snack. That is the order you do things, so it's your algorithm for after school."

It felt good knowing Miss Miata, our new science teacher, had taught us the same thing.

But my favorite part of the day came at the robotics demonstration. A woman who designed cars introduced us to her robot, Dolores. And I saw several people in that session whom I'd met before, including Shania, Shakira, and Alicia. No Venus, though.

Afterward, we all got a chance to talk.

241

"This was really awesome," Alicia said.

Shania looked sheepish. She said to me, "Girl, after being here all day, I'm starting to feel like the way you talk is cool. All these ladies sound more like you than..."

"Us," Shakira said. "And most of them are black and proud!"

We talked about it for a little while. How all these women represented all kinds of neighborhoods, but they made us feel proud to be who we are. It was a powerful message. Even though I didn't like thinking of myself as one of those girls who hugs all the time, I couldn't seem to stop hugging. I embraced the girls and they hugged me back before leaving.

Somehow, I felt like we'd all learned a good lesson.

Later, I talked to so many girls and wrote down so many names, I felt like my hand might fall off. Then we talked to even more grown-ups and wrote down even more names.

When it was all done and we were back in the car, Mr. McShea said he sort of missed me slipping up and calling him "McSweater Vest." He was taking us downtown to eat at his favorite place, Lafayette Coney Island.

We ate chili dogs with mustard and onions, French

fries, and drank Cokes. We sat there and stuffed our faces and stared at the traffic as it crept along the slushy winter streets, watching people walk briskly past, shoulders hunched up into their necks to keep out the cold air.

And we discussed writing and journalism and other careers, too. Like building robots that help make cars!

"I couldn't believe how many people were there. And it was so cool how that woman taught us how to build our own robot and said how she went to Cass Tech. Hey, did you know I wanted to go to Cass Tech, too, but that was back when I wanted to be a cupcake baker and a journalist. And journalism is still way cool, but, I don't know, after today, what if—"

Mr. McShea laughed so hard, he got ketchup in his hipster beard. Red sat shaking her head. "Oh, Justice!" was all she could say.

But when all the laughter was over, it was time to get to work. We left and went to the *Freep*. We had a follow-up story to write.

Putting it all together was a lot of work. It was much harder to write about the meaning of something than to describe all the different things that happened.

A young woman named Trina came over to help out, too. She was a page designer and helped us use the photos that a photographer at the event took to help tell the story. When we were finally done, we hit SEND, and the story went flying to the editor for approval.

We were done.

And I was exhausted.

Time to go home and go to bed!

Reporter's Notebook

Neptune called. Awkward. We watched a movie together online. *Star Wars: The Force Awakens.* He applauded every time a Wookiee appeared on screen! Then we talked and talked, making up our own version of the next Star Wars episode. Mine had a legion of kick-butt black women who used their exceptional computer skills to threaten the empire. Good times.

When you look up "black women in computer science" for research, you get a ton of names. Why did that surprise me???

MELBA ROY MOUTON, was a NASA mathematician called a computer. In the 1960s, she had this big title—Assistant Chief of Research Programs with their Trajectory and Geodynamic division, Whoa!

ANNIE J. EASLEY, computer scientist, mathematician, and rocket scientist who worked for the Lewis Research Center of the National Aeronautics and Space Administration (NASA) and its predecessor, the National Advisory Committee for Aeronautics (NACA) (career started in 1955, as "computer").

DR. EVELYN BOYD GRANVILLE was the second black woman to earn a Ph.D. in mathematics from Yale University (1949). She worked as a Computer Scientist for IBM on the Project Vanguard and Project Mercury space programs, and then for the U.S. Space Technologies Laboratories. She became a longtime professor.

Modern accomplishments by women of color in computer science:

KIMBERLY BRYANT founded San Francisco-based nonprofit Black Girls Code in 2011. Her organization has been responsible for inspiring more than 1,500 girls to work in technology fields such as robotics, video game design, mobile phone application development and computer programming. In 2013, she received the White House Champions of Change for Tech Inclusion award for work to diversify the tech industry.

KYLA MCMULLEN was the first African American woman at the University of Michigan to graduate with a doctorate in computer science. She graduated in 2012. She continues to be an inspiration to young women looking to work in that field. Now, she teaches computer science at the University of Florida as an assistant professor and is the leader of the SoundPad Lab at the University of Florida.

Don't know if I'm falling in love with computer science, but definitely liking the field more!

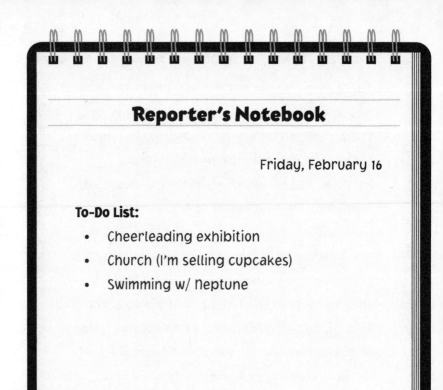

Reporter's Notebook

Friday, February 16

To-Do List:

- Cheerleading exhibition
- Church (I'm selling cupcakes)
- Swimming w/ Neptune

21

Presidents' Day.

Well, almost. No school on Monday, so the mini-movie tribute Click and I organized had to run on Friday.

The entire sixth grade met in the auditorium for morning announcements. We normally waited for Principal Striker to do the morning announcements, then he'd announce our movie and its topic.

Click and I knew that the trick to mini movies was to keep them quick and simple. Kids got the message and laughed. Life went on.

Today was going to be different.

We'd spent many, many hours working on the setup, building structures, and taking pictures. Several different groups of kids had helped with everything from making tiny prop sets to taking the photos to keeping Click's head from exploding during the editing process.

Not an easy task, I might add.

"Good morning, everyone," I said into the mic. "Today we are presenting our movie as a sign of respect and celebration for the lives of all the people who were forced to live in awful conditions because they were being discriminated against. We are celebrating the Fair Housing Act of 1968 and the people who struggled, fought, and even died so that we could live where we want to live.

"But all we have to do is look around us. Open your eyes. People are still living in areas where no one should have to live. Still forced into awful neighborhoods, and ghettos, that are laughed at and ridiculed. For many, there is no easy way out."

I took a breath. Sixth graders quickly get restless, so I didn't want to go on much longer.

"Please check out the *Blueberry* today for my article. Now, without further ado, here is the mini-movie, *Gonna Buy Me a House Someday*, inspired by an award-winning African American playwright, Lorraine Hansberry, and dedicated to the entire sixth-grade class of Blueberry Hills Middle. Thank you!"

A few catcalls and whistles, then the movie started.

We'd done our best to make the pieces look realistic. Since we really couldn't animate the faces like in real movies, Click and his friends did an excellent job of conveying the emotions with music.

Tiny figures, a white couple and a black couple, moved through the colorful neighborhood. Time and again, the black couple was denied a place to live, despite being able to prove they could afford it.

While the movie played and the story became clear, I glanced around the dim auditorium. Several kids' gazes were glued to the screen. It was cool to see how many of them really seemed to be totally into it, the serious message reaching them despite our playful way of getting it across.

"Brianna," Click said, moving up beside me. "You done good, girl!" He leaned down and bumped me playfully with his shoulder. When I looked at his hands, I saw he was holding a LEGO mini-figure. Effortlessly, he removed the figure's head and clicked it up and down a few times.

I☆I☆I☆I

Saturday I awoke to the distinctive odor of wood smoke.

Sleep had been elusive with worrying about today.

251

The exhibition. Was I prepared enough? Would I wind up face-planting in front of a group of other cheerleaders? Or worse: Would I land on my face in front of Neptune?

I dressed in our team's warmup clothes. My body ached in odd places. I was hobbling around like Grandpa after he'd been sitting at the kitchen table too long.

Once I was dressed, I came into the shadowy kitchen, reached for the Pop-Tart box, then drew my hand back.

Dad shuffled in, Grandpa behind him.

"Pop-Tarts? Not from the baking diva herself. Baking chef extraordinaire, Miss Brianna Justice!" Grandpa chuckled.

I scowled.

Daddy said, "Hmm...that doesn't look like a happy cheerleader this morning."

They went on with their jokes and I decided to ignore the premade pastry. Suddenly, I had no appetite. What I did have was a humongous case of stage fright.

I would like to say that after the recent success of the story I wrote with Red, not to mention the positive response the school had to the mini-movie project, my confidence was at an all-time high. And trust me, that's pretty high.

However, as my brain churned with dance moves, kicks, flips, turns, stretches, and everything else that went into the exhibition, I couldn't stop the knocking in my knees and the dryness in my mouth.

Our team met downtown at the dance school, then we boarded a bus and headed across the state, not stopping until we arrived at the biggest high school I'd ever seen. We were in Ann Arbor, where the University of Michigan was located. The parking lot was a sea of buses.

I sneaked a glance at Red and she glanced at me and we glanced back and forth at each other.

Stunt rehearsal turned my empty stomach into a sour, gurgling mess. And what else had my intestines in a knot?

Two words—*LOCKER ROOM*!

Sure, I had changed clothes in front of other girls before. I wasn't a baby. I had P.E. However, this wasn't gym class at good ol' Blueberry Hills Middle. And the girls filling up the enormous space were not shy little sixth and seventh graders, either.

This was like some huge dressing room area with hundreds of girls. I couldn't help gawking. Then I turned around because I didn't want anyone to think, you know, I was checking them out.

But I am checking them out.

And it wasn't just the stranger girls who had me buggin'. It was our girls, too. When they peeled out of their warmups and put on their real uniforms, it was like—*BOOM!*—above the neck, kid. Below the neck, GROWN-UP WOMAN.

You know what was below my neck?

More neck.

It was horrifying.

"Psst!" I half hissed, half whispered to Red. When I turned to her, she was bent over, carefully lifting the sparkly silver uniform top over her head. She wore a bra so pale, it was the same nude color as her flesh. Her underpants matched. God, I felt like a third grader. I didn't even think about that. My non-bra was one of those things you get that have the little spaghetti straps and lies softly across your chest. Mine had butterflies. *Isn't that sweet?* BUTTERFLIES! My outward wardrobe had definitely become more serious, befitting an up-and-coming business woman.

My undies, not so much.

"No one told me we'd have to change clothes in front of...so many girls," I said.

She shrugged. "In dance, you get used to it."

If that wasn't terrifying enough, however, while we practiced, we heard a commotion coming from inside the auditorium.

One of the girls said, "It's some kind of celebrity, I think. People are trying to talk to him or something."

Now my heart did a kick. Neptune. Had to be. Numbness tingled in my legs and lips and arms and fingers. I wanted to freak out. Say something.

No time. Too busy working on my balance, body control, flexibility, and squeezing my butt tight.

"Brianna, come here please," Coach T. called out before it was time for us to go on. I could feel myself shaking inside.

Still, my heart thudded to the bam-bam beat. Sweat tickled my hairline. No junior executive bun today. Instead, my hair was gelled and brushed back, held with a tightly wound rubber band. The ponytail was fluffed and sparkled with some sort of hair glitter one of the girls had sprayed on.

"Yes," I said, voice cracking. Despite how much fun it was to see her a few weeks ago at the SheCodes event, she still kept yelling at me for two weeks straight about my form, stamina, and intensity.

"I wanted to let you know how proud Kristy and I are of you," she said, causing me to about fall over with relief. "I know I challenged you in the beginning, but that was because I see so much potential in you."

"T-thanks, Coach T.," I stammered.

She went on. "We need strong, smart girls like you in competitive cheer. We need you to know you can be physically fit and scientifically inclined and ready to take on the world. Go get 'em, girl!"

Inside the gym, the music changed tempo. The beat dropped hard and the rhythm of my heart followed. I reached out, grabbed my coach, and hugged her.

"Calm down, honey," she said soothingly with a laugh. "I'm still going to ride you like I do all the other girls. But we just wanted you to know how proud we are."

Our team hit the floor. I was set up side by side with teammates, ready to do battle.

Tracy said with a grudging smile, "Get that scorpion, girl. I got you!"

Everything happened so fast. Going from one position to the next required so much concentration. We had done this routine over and over and over. I honestly had been doing it in my sleep. But an electric thread of terror coursed through my veins as I feared forgetting a step. While writing our story for the paper, I had been convinced award-winning journalism was much tougher than competitive cheer.

Now I wasn't at all sure.

When it was time to go into the air, I sucked in my breath, tightened the muscles in my belly and butt, and locked my legs. Red, also hoisted into the air, gave me a quick smile. With one fluid motion, I did the scorpion stretch.

And... then it was over!

Elation prickled my skin. I felt so happy. So alive. Then, right before we ran off the center mat, I caught a glimpse of a familiar face.

Neptune!

All during the performance I'd been afraid to look into the crowd. Now I looked, and when I did, I laughed out loud. Sitting beside him and his Secret Service escorts was my family. Mom was all dressed up in her FBI clothes, which meant she was on duty.

Part of his protection detail?

Katy waved enthusiastically and I waved back. When my gaze met Neptune's, we both smiled shyly. Okay, so we'd agreed beforehand to nod to each other, but not make a big fuss.

The last thing I wanted was to cause a stir in the press with rumors of dating the POTUS's nephew. After all, I was in the media now. I had a reputation to protect.

I☆I☆I☆I

Sunday.

A mild snowstorm hit the city overnight. The world turned from slushy dirty snow to frozen white once again.

Of course, floating on a plastic ring in a pool heated to eighty-five degrees made the winter storm seem far, far away. Neptune was also floating on a colorful inner tube, black swim goggles pulled on top of his head. My hair was parted and plaited down the middle. School was out the next day, Presidents' Day. I was glad to have the day off. I'd wash my hair tomorrow. Today, well, perhaps Neptune would get the full Wookiee experience!

I stared up through a glass ceiling that revealed a treacherously pale winter sky. Wind rose and every so often rattled the sides of the hotel. We paid that howling wind almost no attention.

"So you enjoyed the robotics, huh?" Neptune asked for the fourth or fifth time.

"Yeah, yeah. I get it. You were right about the conference and—me. Maybe...just maybe, I might want to be a little more open to what I could learn about my future. Don't go getting ahead of yourself, though!"

We both laughed.

Neptune reached out and tugged my inner tube until we were floating side by side.

"So, Wook, what have you decided? About moving to D.C., I mean?"

I sighed. Mom and I hadn't talked about it since that day after school. Still, at home I could feel her and Dad stealing glances my way, like they were trying to look inside my head and read my thoughts. "Well, she says she hasn't decided yet, but in her heart, I know Mom's all set to go. It would mean a lot to her."

"So..."

When I looked at him, for one crazy, horrible second I thought for sure I would burst into tears. Instead, I drew a deep breath.

"So..." I began, "when we leave here today I'm going to insist she take that promotion. A woman has a right to advance in her career, you know?"

"Oh, I do." Neptune grinned, then, becoming more serious, he asked, "Are you cool with it? Or are you sad?"

The donut-shaped floaty pushed lower into the water as I lay back. Red and I had talked about it. Instead of making a bunch of promises about keeping in touch later, we just decided—if Mom takes the job—to do as much stuff as we can while we're together.

We even decided maybe we would take Miss Addy up on her offer and travel north to Mackinac Island for the summer.

Eyes still closed, I said, "Not sad. Well, yes, sad. But more so about what I'll be leaving behind."

I opened my eyes and looked at him. I said, "But maybe I'm looking forward to new experiences."

Neptune's face was inches from mine as I stared up toward the ceiling. I smiled. He smiled. It felt good knowing I'd have a friend in D.C.

Still, when he cut his eyes to one side and leaned in for a super-quick smooch, I saw stars for a minute.

"Time for a snack break!" he declared.

We raced to the pool's edge and pulled ourselves up onto the deck. That was when I noticed a silver tray with a bell-shaped lid, like you get for room service.

"I had a special snack prepared for you!" he said. But the way he said it, it was like he was in first grade or something.

"What is it?" I asked.

He went to the table and whipped away the lid. On the tray was a large plate filled with Oreo cookies.

"You like?" He waved his hand past the plate like we were on a game show and he was the wacky host.

I punched him right in his arm. "You are NOT funny!" I said, but I was laughing really hard. Of course, after the whole Oreo thing at Price, I had told him about it. He said if he had a dollar for every time someone either in person or on the Internet called him Oreo he'd be a billionaire. He'd said, "Wook, you can't let nobody steal the goodness of milk's favorite cookie!"

He began laughing so hard that he snorted. We each lifted a glass of milk from the tray, grabbed a cookie, then tapped the cookies together in a toast.

When we reached for our last cookies, instead of dunking them, we both shoved the whole cookie in our mouths and made googly eyes at each other. Then he shoved me into the pool and fell in beside me. I nearly snorked my cookie!

"You're silly!" I said, pushing him away.

"Okay, seriously? You know I'm looking forward to it," he said. His cookie was gone. Now I couldn't help noticing how beautiful his eyes were. Especially with flecks of Oreo stuck to his cheek below.

"Really?" I said. I felt dizzy—excited, nervous, a little weird.

At least until he said, "Sure! I want to show my friends that I haven't been making it up. I know a real-live Wookiee from Star Wars!"

With that, I shoved him this time and we were racing around the pool.

Just the two of us.

And his protection detail.

And somewhere in the shadows, dear ol' Mom.

Afterward we would go to the hotel sweet shop for more dessert. Might be the perfect time to tell Mom I wanted us to do what was best for everyone, not just me.

Then it would be time for a double-scoop sundae.

I☆I☆I☆I

Acknowledgments

I would like to thank Dr. Jakita Thomas at Auburn University, who offered excellent tips and words of wisdom to young lady scientists. A special thank-you to Dr. Quincy Brown, Ph.D., Program Director for STEM Education Research at the American Association for the Advancement of Science (AAAS), for her thoughtful input and insight into what it means to be a girl of math and science. Any mistakes or missteps are completely mine and not the fault of Dr. Thomas or Dr. Brown. And my good friend Audra Burch, reporter for the *New York Times*. You ladies gave me excellent role models upon which to build my story.